No Such Thing as Ghosts

by

S.F.L. Jefferies

The Haunting of Pinedale High

Cover Art by *The Wild Rose Press, Inc.*

The Wild Rose Press, Inc.
PO Box 708
Adams Basin, NY 14410-0708
Visit us at www.thewildrosepress.com

Publishing History
First Edition, 2025
Trade Paperback ISBN 978-1-5092-6122-2
Digital ISBN 978-1-5092-6123-9

Published in the United States of America

Dedication

To anyone who's never fit in

Acknowledgements

It's been a long writing journey, filled with far more challenges than I could have ever imagined.

This book would not be possible without three amazing longstanding supporters.

To my fellow author, Romy Sommer, your words of encouragement meant that when the call came for this series, I didn't ignore it.

Okay, I did ignore it, at first. But it tick tick ticked in the realms of my subconscious. "What if?"

"What if?" turned into "why not?" one Sunday morning long run with my sister, Kate, who pointed out it's ghosts, it's YA, and it's everything I love. *Duh.*

I turned in my synopsis for this book to my marvellous, patient, and eagle-eyed editor, ELF, who to be fair, has read some of my manuscripts that needed a lot of work or even life support. But this one turned into an acceptance.

There are no words enough to express my thanks, my gratitude and my appreciation.

Chapter 1

First Day Jitters

Do you ever get that feeling that everyone's staring at you?

Weighing you up, judgy mc-judgy and then some? I'm trying to pretend that's not the case, but let's face it, Dad's assertion that jeans and a T-shirt are "just fine" is an out-and-out lie.

Right now, I'm pining for my much-loathed school uniform with the thick green tights—sorry, stockings, no, *pantyhose*, is that right?—green pleated skirt, and basic blouse that turned yellow under my pits. Did it suck? Yes. Big time. I raged every chance I had about its polyester ability to squash individuality and personal expression.

And now, all around me are cute little asymmetrical tops, crop tops, and high-waisted jeans. The very items I already have, sitting in a crate somewhere over the Atlantic, moving with all the speed of a constipated snail.

My vintage designer pants, oversized denim jacket, and strappy top, while a loose interpretation of my father's recommendation, are decidedly too much here.

Back at home, I'd be dead-on.

Yeah, but Pinedale is not Putney, London, mate.

Hence, all the eyeballs scoping me out.

My stomach's totally twisted, my nerves shredded

1

down to raw stubs, and even laser UV-glued nails can't survive my chewing habit.

I get it. I do.

I don't even have to open my mouth for others to realize I'm not from here.

Maybe it's the way I walk or wear my hair, or maybe I'm transmitting some kind of vibe they can tune into.

I look like the freak I am.

The instructions said to wait at Pinedale High's entrance.

Everyone knows everyone, and I bet they're all up in everyone's business. It's a small town. Dad grew up here. He doesn't speak about it much, but the fact that he chose to come back must mean something. He never gave me an actual reason why we're here. I assumed it was to put as much distance between him and everything surrounding my mother's death. A whole-ass ocean is a pretty big distance, if you ask me.

I think there's another, bigger reason.

The minutes are ticking by, and my fingers are twitching. Pretty much everyone's clocked me. Stranger danger. My thumb's working overtime while I scroll through my feed. My headphones are back home, where I left them by my bed. Even a tutorial on full-glam '90s makeup can't erase the anxiety that's eating away at me.

How do they school here? They have subjects I've never heard of, like social studies. What is that? Learning how to make small talk? There're also a bunch of clubs, like dance club and sports. We called it "games" back home, and we mostly whacked around a hockey stick or tumbled on a mat.

And this school sprawls and takes up acres of space. There's even a whole-ass wood behind it. A *wood.*

Mental. We had to drive out for kilometers (sorry, *miles*) to get near an actual wood, and that wood looked like it belonged in an animated movie. This wood...doesn't. It flanks the school like a dark, deep shadow waiting to yank it up and cart it away.

That wood's staring at me. I can feel it. It's giving me the shivers. The goose-bumps kind that break out on the back of your neck. You could get lost in that wood, and I bet no one would find you for days.

A yell pierces the air, bursting it bright like a balloon.

I almost drop my phone.

Three guys are showing off near the parking lot. They're look-at-me-loud, but no one's really paying attention to them. They're dressed in black leather jackets and jeans like it's a uniform, hair slicked back in a style I can't remember seeing anywhere other than on the classic movie channel. They're guffawing over something, slapping each other on the back, and what can only be described as playing the fool. One turns in my direction, and oh, get this—he's smoking. A *cigarette*. Who smokes cigarettes anymore? It's like screaming, "Hey, I'm a rebel, notice me."

Do they think they look...*cool*?

And here I was worrying about my vintage pants, and these guys are playing the retro card in spades.

Weird.

'Cos, like I say, no one's giving them even a second of attention.

Maybe it's a small-town thing? My nerves are still shredding my insides, but I can't keep my gaze off the three guys exchanging old-school vibes. One of them, a greasy blond, has books, but he's keeping them tucked out of view from the others. The smoker focuses on blowing perfect *O*'s. The third keeps adjusting and readjusting his jacket collar, pulling it up with his thumbs.

Just when I think I'm imagining things, a slip of a guy slinks past them, keeping a lower profile than a celeb put on blast. He almost clears them too.

Gotcha! Smoker Guy has him, arm swiftly round his shoulders, corralling him back until he's in a headlock, escape impossible. Smoker Guy's features are cut into an ugly smile. He's loving every moment of his captive's squirm for freedom.

Dad mentioned that Pinedale's supposed to be supportive, inclusive, all that good stuff. Someone forgot to tell these guys.

Jacket Boy rifles through their prisoner's pockets, pulling them inside out and pocketing the contents.

A couple walks past them, hand in hand, oblivious. My insides turn uneasily. So it's one of *those* schools. Do what you like on the inside, so long as the outside picture is all sunshine, lollipops, and rainbows.

Or these guys are really nasty.

I get the shivers again.

If anything, Smoker Guy's pulled his prey even tighter. I wince. Is he going to frogmarch him to a second location? Why is no one doing anything? Here and there, a student will scuttle past, averting their eyes. But that doesn't explain the others with their nothing-to-see-here vibe. It's almost as if—

"Are you Lila Brown?"

The voice interrupts my train of thought that has careened clean off the track and straight down the hill.

A pair of angry, bespectacled eyes glare at me. "Lila

Brown, the new kid?"

"I—"

"Here, take this." He shoves a pile of books my way. "Here's your timetable. The office gave you a hard copy." Somehow, he made that sound like a swear word. "Class starts at eight. I've been assigned to you for your first month here. I'll show you to your locker."

And he was off! Charging through the students, a man on a mission, the athletic type forced to mingle with the less well-coordinated.

The books weigh me down, and I battle to keep up with him. "Assigned to me? Do you mean like a buddy?"

He didn't even turn round. "Keep up, we're gonna be late, and I've got a record to maintain."

My feet nearly slip out of my shoes. My new "buddy" is heading straight toward those three jerks. Making a beeline for them, if anything. They've given up on their original quarry and are now looking around for fresh sport.

I duck-paddle my feet to keep up. "Those guys, they weren't very nice to—"

"Class starts at eight on the dot. You can choose to be late one month from now, got it?"

"Yes, but perhaps we should…" My words die in my throat.

Smoker Guy makes direct eye contact. And holds. The glint in his eye is anything but friendly.

But my buddy keeps with the pace—things to do, places to be, death warrants to sign.

As if in slow motion, Smoker Guy extends his boot-clad foot, catching buddy boy mid-calf, and sends him sprawling.

Chapter 2

My Buddy Joe

My buddy hits the decks with all his weight behind him. I half expect to see the concrete roll up where he's plowed into it. His glasses bounce from his face.

Smoker Guy picks them up, examines them, and snaps them clean in half before tossing them back toward his victim.

They positively howl with laughter, a mean, cruel sound that kicks in the ribs.

I can't stop myself. "Why, you..."

"What?" challenges Smoker Guy. Up close, he has all the charm of a snarling rat, his incisors neat, sharp, and bared.

An old-fashioned smell that reminds me of my grandfather follows him. Slightly spicy, slightly sweet, something I can't put my finger on. My gaze drifts to his hair which is black and slickly coated in gel, so much gel. Too much gel.

His face pushes into my space. "Boys, it's another arrival from Halford." He gives a grin that doesn't reach his eyebrows. "You wanna come here, you stick with your own kind, you got that?"

He pauses for dramatic effect that, let me tell you, works. I swallow back any thoughts of putting him straight. Halford? My own kind? What does that even mean? From what I've seen in my whole few minutes at Pinedale High, it's all about the diversity. Sure, for some, that's a threat more than a reality, but where the heck is Halford?

I can see the blackheads on his nose.

The guy is twice my size, and he's all snap and crackle with aggro that I have no intention of testing out. Yeah, I got it. My own kind. Whatever he said. Who am I to argue?

He gives a smirk. "See you around."

I sure hope not.

Smoker Guy and his two stooges stroll away from their crime scene.

The blond takes out a comb and fixes his hair. For real.

He glances back at me, and so help me, for a split second, I swear he wants to say something. There's a pause in his step. A contemplation.

And then he joins the others.

A grunt reminds me I'm not alone.

Buddy boy snarls at his broken glasses. His palms are loaded with dirt and grit where he tried to break his fall.

I bet his knees hurt badly too. That was some drop.

"Are you okay?" I offer him my hand to help get him back on his feet.

He ignores me like a stop sign and pushes upward.

I don't need to be an expert in social studies to recognize the guy is burning with embarrassment.

He picks up his bag and readjusts it over his shoulder.

Smoker Guy and his mates pace away from the crime scene with swagger rather than speed. Buddy boy can easily catch up to them.

But he makes no attempt to retaliate. No fist throwing or epic name-calling or even running to bop that jerk straight on the nose.

If I were a guy, I would've tried something. Especially if I was a big guy like this one. An athletic type. I bet he packed a whole six-pack with extras under his shirt.

Instead, he gathers himself together and acts like nothing's happened, no biggie, nothing-to-see-here-folks. Except for the broken glasses.

I offer my sympathies. "It seemed like a pretty mean thing to do."

He frowns then. Annoyed even. "I tripped. It happens."

Say what? "Tripped?"

There's nothing buddy-buddy about this guy now. Not that there was much to start with. His face reads open hostility. "Let's get to class."

"But those guys…"

"We're going to—"

"Be late, yes, I heard you."

Way to go, Lila. I haven't even got to my first class yet, and already I've somehow made, count them—one, two, three, *four* enemies. That had to be a record.

It was the accent. Maybe I sounded posh? Or stuck up? I expect a healthy dose of mockery. I do. But really, it's the way we say our vowel sounds that are different. Otherwise, it's all the same English. Except for some of the words. *Most* of the words.

Buddy boy stops short in front of a row of lockers. "Look, let me get something straight with you. I don't have the time to buddy anyone. It's football season, and the coach has made it clear I have an important role in keeping the team motivated."

You could have knocked me down with a feather. This guy was a team motivator? Talk about hidden talents.

He hasn't finished his lecture yet. "I also have a GPA to maintain."

I refrain from asking what that is. It sounds important, though. Maybe it was like the GCSEs? A final exam we have to take that determines our entire future. A feeling of dread weighs me down. Getting through each day is challenge enough without having to consider what I want to be doing for the REST OF MY LIFE.

The concept of such a thought is so heavy it's like loading up my pockets with cement blocks.

He bangs his fist on a locker door, which springs open like in the movies. "This is yours."

"Oh wow. Do I keep all my books in here?"

He doesn't answer me.

I suspect he determined sarcasm rather than inquiry. "You don't have to babysit me. I'm a big girl. I can figure it out," I reassure him. Seriously though, do I need to get a padlock?

He sighs. "That's not the policy here. We support each other."

If he was well-versed in irony, he wasn't letting on.

"First class is Biology. You'll need to take this book here." He points to one with a photo of a big-bellied frog on the front. "And then it's Math. This one." Blue-covered and dog-eared.

"Did you get an 'A' in Social Studies?" I couldn't resist.

"The hall pass is so you can go to the office to meet

with the counsellor to make sure you're not crazy."

My skin prickles at that. An uneasiness sinks straight into my bones, and I'm back to thinking about that deep, dark wood surrounding me right now.

He must have seen my inherent enthusiasm because his tone eases up. "Don't worry, they don't think you're crazy," he reassures me. "It's just a formality."

Yeah. Right.

It had nothing to do with anything.

The counsellor? My thoughts cloud over with every past misdemeanor I could have committed, real or imagined. Unless, of course, it was to talk about my particular elephant in the room. That which would not be named.

Crazy.

That's what they'd called my mother. Crazy. And not in a good way. If there was a good way to be called crazy.

The bell rings.

Buddy boy starts moving. "Lunch is at eleven. You can bring your own, but if you eat at the cafeteria, don't eat the chicken fingers. They're like…not good."

"Noted." I scamper after him. Do I sense a reprieve? A potential olive branch?

He high-fives a guy with a hundred nose piercings in the corridor and says he'll "catch them later."

A girl blows him a kiss, which he pretends to catch and tuck in his pocket.

I mean, really.

And a younger guy shouts in his direction, "Loved that pass."

We arrive at a set of double doors, and he announces, "This is the biology lab."

Any thoughts about olive branches vanish.

I attempt the conversational pleasantries that have been missing from our interaction. "And what do I call you?"

"Call me?"

"Your name is?"

"Joe."

"Ah. Nice to meet you, Joe."

He's already eased his way to the lab table near the back of the room.

So much for the buddy system.

For a ghost of a second, I swear I see another girl take my place next to him. It must have been my imagination though, because when I look again, it's an empty seat. And my buddy, Joe.

With much reluctance, I sit alongside him and gear up for a bumpy ride.

Chapter 3

Into the Woods

"Class, we have a new student."

Thirty pairs of eyes turn and gawp at me.

The biology teacher delivers the line I've been dreading. "Tell us something about yourself, Lila."

Here we go. Show and tell. Did I mention how much I hate public speaking?

I push to my feet from the lab stool that looks like it survived the Ark. To wave or not to wave, that is the question. I venture a smile that stops halfway. "Heya, I'm Lila. Good to be here." My voice cracks somewhere in the middle of my delivery.

My mind draws a total blank.

I sit down again.

There's an awkward pause. Do I stand back up? The teacher's eyebrows are raised, a *was-that-it*? gesture. It was, sir, it was. There's no reason to draw unnecessary attention my way. It would lead to questions I don't want to answer. Like, why are you really here?

I drop my gaze, hopeful Mr. Teacher will take the hint and let it go.

"Lila's moved here from London, in England." He gives one of those on/off smiles. "Welcome to Pinedale High, Lila."

It's been quite the welcome already.

I mumble my thanks, hoping the spotlight will now shift elsewhere.

Joe shuffles in his seat next to me. He's already laid out his books, his tablet, a pen, a notebook, and his phone, which he's slipped under the notebook.

For someone who seems obsessive about a perfect record and punctuality, he seems to be flexible on the interpretation of school rules. Like the no-phones policy.

"We're exploring local ecology, Lila," explained Mr. Teacher. "We've also looked at fungi and ferns. You can catch up in your free time."

I nod. Sounds exhilarating.

"Which brings me to today's lesson. If you could all pair up, preferably with your original lab partners."

There's a rumble of movement as one or two students switch seats. I try to find something to do with my hands. Did they have to do pick-a-partner on my first day? Memories of being last picked for hockey jostle for my attention.

Joe grunts in my direction. "Yeah, you're with me."

I wait for my brain to come up with a witty, wisecracking retort, but it remains stubbornly silent. If I wait five minutes, it will think of something, but the opportunity will have passed. Don't you hate when that happens?

The lab is three times the size of the one we had in my old school, with ceramic sinks lining the walls. Each table has a Bunsen burner, ready and waiting, and the whole place pongs of sulfur. There's also a chill in the air that keeps brushing past me. I'm so glad I have my oversized distressed denim jacket that offers maximum style and minimum warmth.

The class is all paired up, and the chatter is peaking.

Mr. Teacher pulls the class back into orbit. "Right, class. For this task, you'll need to go into the woods and select a number of soil samples. Please do not take from the same area. You'll have to choose three locations, at least a mile apart from each other. And please don't use the area closest to the school. Dig deep." He has a slow smile at his own joke. "Explore. Find areas where there are multiple plant species, and that's not out by the road."

The woods? Soil samples? Why didn't he ask us to climb a tree or play with bugs for good measure?

Alas, he wasn't finished.

"Choose the optimum soil from your samples."

My fingers were already twitching at the thought of all that dirt under my fingernails.

"Then, using locally sourced plants —not from the woods—build a terrarium. There are instructions in your online portal as well as in the handouts, so no excuses. You have three weeks to complete the task, and no, class, we're not taking a meander out there during class time. And yes, you have to complete the task in full and on time."

So, I have to go into the woods with Mr. Personality here and pick up dirt after school. Got it.

"Take a minute or two to discuss your approach, class."

Instantly, the lab buzzes with activity. Stools squeak, bodies move, and the hum of chatter rises once more.

This teacher is clearly a firm believer in teamwork and group projects.

I turn to Joe. "Do we have to take turns as short-order cook at the local caf for food technology?"

He blinks at me. "I don't understand what you're

saying." His blank stare confirms this.

"It was a joke," I explain.

"Yeah, so environmental science is kind of my thing." He's as serious as an undertaker with a body on the slab. "This type of project is exactly what I need to further my applications when the time comes."

"Your applications?"

"To college."

"But that's not for a few years…"

He tilts his head to the side like I'm mad for even suggesting it. "Competition is crazy. You need to think ahead to get ahead."

"It's an aquarium," I point out.

"It's a *terrarium,* and it's in line with my future career as an environmentalist."

He's taped his broken glasses back together, and right now, he's the picture of an insane scientist. All he needs is to ruffle up his hair and don a white jacket. Who are you heading into those creepy woods with, Lila? Ah, my intense "buddy" Joe, mad scientist extraordinaire. Good times at Pinedale High. "An environmentalist and a football team motivator. Got it."

He's poring over his calendar app, which is chockablock with activity. "I've got practice Tuesdays and Wednesdays, so we'll have to schedule for Thursday afternoon. Or we could meet up before school. If you can get here on time. Saturdays are out."

"Totally." I nod. "They're like so last season."

He fixes me with his gaze from behind two lenses and half a roll of Scotch tape. "Thursday afternoon, then."

"It's a date!" I lean heavily on the sarcasm.

I don't get it. This guy breezed past those creeps

earlier like nothing happened. Ignored them entirely. He still hasn't addressed the grit in his palms. But he's giving me gears for no reason at all. I didn't ask to have a buddy. I didn't ask him to be my buddy. I didn't ask to come to this school either.

So far, none of the choices here are mine.

He's now texting under the table.

I don't look the same. I don't wear the right clothes. I don't say the right things. So far, so good.

Hi, I'm Lila, and I'm here because my father needs to go back to familiar things. But nothing's familiar. Everything's different.

The teacher keeps eyeballing me.

He seems the anxious type, rocking on his heels.

His gaze flitters over the students.

Bet he's zoning out. It's been longer than two minutes. The pair in front of me are dissecting the latest episode of that Regency romance series. Why can't I be at that table? The costumes in that show are out-of-this-world amazing. All those flounces and frills and tucks and pleats. And the way they use color to show the different houses, well—

"Lila B?" A woman's voice echoes through the lab.

All eyes swivel to me once more.

This is so cringe, I can't even.

"The counsellor will see you now."

Perfect. No choice but to brazen out any social leprosy. Why didn't they say I'd accidentally peed myself and left a puddle on my chair?

Do I take my books with? Do I leave them with Joe? I pick up my hall pass.

I breeze out of there. Cool as eff.

I consider blowing a kiss goodbye to Joe. And his

terrarium.

"I promise not to miss you," I say.
Could today get any worse?

Chapter 4

True confessions

"Lila B? Is that what you prefer to be called?"

The super-old woman in front of me has a falsie that's come unglued. It's lifted at the edge and is threatening to take flight. I'm transfixed. Part of me wants to reach over and push it down, see if it will stick again. Eyelash glue isn't tacky like that though. It's more one-and-done.

A guidance counsellor who wears false eyelashes. In-ter-es-ting.

There's a long silence.

She said something to me, didn't she? "I beg your pardon?"

"Is Lila B your preferred name?"

"Yes, ma'am."

"It's Mrs. Linton."

She scribbles in her notebook, and I try and fail not to focus on her errant eyelash strip. Look at the way it rises and falls. How is it not driving her nuts? It must be smacking into her upper eyelid or drifting into her vision.

I drag my attention away from her eyelashes.

Every few seconds, behind her office door, there's the sound of someone walking past. It's distracting. Especially if that someone's talking too. The ebb and flow of movement has me sitting tighter in my chair.

What if another student knocks on the door?

Going to the counsellor back home was like announcing you had a highly infectious, contagious, socially stigmatizing disease.

I never went to the counsellor. Ever.

And here I am. First day.

"So, Lila B…" Mrs. Linton leans back on her chair that groans. "You're our first student to transfer here from the U.K. I hope we're not too scary."

For a second, my thoughts turn to those guys in the leather jackets. They were scary. Mean scary. Strange scary.

She swoops back toward her desk and steeples her fingers together. "Your father told us about your mother. I'm sorry for your loss."

Those particular words feel like grey ash. They mean nothing at all, but they settle round me in a haze, reminding me I can't forget even if I wanted to. "Thank you."

"He also told me…"

Here it comes. I brace myself.

"…that she spent some time in a mental institution. For schizophrenia."

"That's not what my mother called it."

"Oh?"

Damn, fell straight into her trap on that one. "It was more like hypervigilance."

"Hypervigilance? Tell me more about that."

I'd rather gargle razor blades. My mother was gone, and it hurt in a way that was always raw, always ready to trip me up. But what gut punches me the most is thinking about what she went through before she died. The agony of the living part. The men in their white coats. The medications. The daily misery of simple existence.

I don't want to take a trip down that particular memory lane, not here, not with this stranger, and not in this room with its drafty corners and reek of thousand-year-old unwashed carpet.

I shrug. "She was more sensitive than most people. She noticed things. That's all."

Mrs. Linton peers at me, her false eyelash strip fluttering. "Lila B, if you need to talk at any time… If you're feeling like you need support to help you through this transition, I'm always here, as a safe space."

"Thank you."

"Making a huge move like you and your father did can be very stressful, and then with your bereavement as well…it can be a tough time for you."

The prickle behind my eyeballs kicks in. I look up, forcing the emotion to take a hike back into the bottom of my belly or wherever it normally hides.

The noise outside the corridor swells again. Like a herd of students whooping and cheering and shouting. It's a welcome distraction.

Mrs. Linton switches back to her paperwork, her momentary warmth slipping away like the sun on a winter's evening. "You'll have to pick up Spanish. I see here you did French."

"*Oui.*"

"They're similar enough. Do you have any interests, hobbies, or any idea of what your future career path will be?"

Mrs. Linton and Joe. Same texting group.

"Or which colleges you'd like to attend?"

"I haven't given it a lot of thought." Pardon me if my adolescence has so far been punctuated with visits to sanitoriums and funeral homes. It didn't leave a lot of time for planning THE REST OF MY LIFE.

Mrs. Linton runs her finger down what must be my previous report card. "Your grades are good. Though I see you battle with English."

"I speak it just fine. It's the writing and the reading part I don't love. All those words."

She doesn't smile. "You can always stay on in the summer to catch up."

Yay. Please, can I? "Thank you."

"How are you getting along with your buddy?"

"Joe's great. Such a fun guy."

"Yeah, he's one of our finest."

Time for me to raise my eyebrows. "Yeah, must be difficult for him with all that pressure—"

A loud slam echoes from behind her door.

"Sounds like someone rammed a trolley into the wall," I say. "It's quite the railway station you have out there. How do you concentrate with all that chatter?"

Mrs. Linton tilts her chin.

I correct myself. "Shopping cart. Trolley. I keep forgetting."

"I didn't hear anything."

Right now, I could hear an earring drop on a cushion. My insides turn to liquid. "Oh?"

Her attention on me is at one hundred percent.

The heat blooms in my cheeks. I sit on my hands. "My mistake."

She takes her sweet time to answer, and every word is measured. "They put the guidance counsellor's office here because it's close to the library. It doesn't get as much foot traffic as the media center. And it's right next to the principal's office. That means it's quiet. It's one of the quieter spots in the whole school."

Of course, she could be so used to all of that racket that she doesn't even hear it anymore. Like my friend, Jo, who lives in the Heathrow flight path. They shout at each other every time a plane flies over. To them, shouting is normal speaking volume.

I think on my feet and stumble. "I was making a joke. Sarcasm. Lowest form of wit. It's the nerves. First day and all. In the counsellor's office."

Her tone switches. "Nothing to be nervous of at all. I'm always here for the students."

The students. Not *my* students. Should that make a difference?

"But you do need to start thinking about your future. We prefer our students to have a goal they can work toward. Maybe there's a club you'd like to join? Are you into sports?"

"No, and they're not into me either."

Her mouth twitches. "There's the school play? Or choir? Perhaps you could try pottery or debate?"

I don't suppose trawling the net for vintage designer wear is on her list? "Maybe an art class?"

"There's photography. You can sign up for that. Better still, I'll sign you up. While you find your feet."

I groan inwardly. I can think of nothing worse. Wait, I can. Digging up dirt behind the school with Captain Fantastic.

"It will get better, Lila B. Have some faith."

Mrs. Linton then stamps my hall pass and sends me back off to class.

I look at the timetable. Ah, my heart is filled to bursting.

English.

Chapter 5

The Bruno Brothers

Outside Mrs. Linton's office, there's not a single soul. Maybe I did imagine all those noises? Or I exaggerated them? Sure, one or two kids probably clattered past, not whole gangs of them.

That's total BS. I heard what I heard.

I brush away my unease.

First days are always stressful. It's nerves on newness on stress on anxiety on twisted guts on heartburn.

First days are all about being a beginner. Unsure, uncertain, a complete newbie. No one is expected to get everything right on the first day. That's madness.

There's a perfectly rational explanation for everything.

Someone tell that to the pretzel in my stomach.

I do have a problem, though.

I don't have a GPS, so where the English class is, I don't know. And there's no one to ask.

I wander down a corridor that's lined with lockers. It looks similar to the one Joe directed me to earlier. Similar but not the same. Cleaner, tidier even. More grown up?

There's a girl's toilet. *Bathroom.*

I push on the door and am immediately enveloped

by the strong smell of disinfectant and cherry-flavored vape. It could knock a helicopter clean out of the sky.

A second later, I'm not sure who's more surprised – me or the near-six-foot giant in front of the mirror rocking an amazing '80s vibe with waist-length crimped hair and green eyeliner. They're painting their mouth black with what looks like a marker pen.

There's an awkward pause, as if I'd caught them in the act. Of what? Crimes of fashion?

"Wouldn't lipstick work better?" Any number of fashion houses do black. "Mascara? A kohl pencil?"

They look at me, one plucked eyebrow arched. A study in planes and angles. Too late, I remember that unsolicited advice is criticism. But really, a marker pen?

"Now why didn't I think of that!" There's no snide to their voice. "Mascara. Ob-viously."

"Obvs."

"Love the accent, luv."

"Love the outfit." I gawp at the retro gear in front of me. Tights—sorry, *leggings*—with stirrups—stirrups! A boxy, stonewashed denim jacket littered with zips and a pink bubble skirt. "Where'd you get this stuff?"

"Stole it." Their tone is dead serious. Then, a wink. "The usual mall stores. It's how you put it together. But enough about me, let's talk about those pants. Now, they're awesome."

I can't help it, and I do a twirl. "Pirate pants. Designer."

"Designer punk." They check out the label. "And you're talking about fashion royalty." Their jaw drops in awed amazement. "Color me impressed. You'll appreciate this. Look!" Under their jacket, men's suspenders hold up their skirt. "From Paris's *enfant terrible*. Just like Madonna in that movie."

Sure, I've heard of Madonna. Didn't she sing that one song? They must really be big into the '80s. Even their blush placement is more 1984 than 2024. I have to admire the commitment to their vintage craft. "Your makeup is so on point."

"Thanks...I think. I like to explore the area between new romantic and new wave." They take a step back from the mirror and adjust their skirt and jacket, pouting black-markered lips.

"Like the music?"

"For sure like the music. I even tried boil-on-the-stove flaxseed gel to get my hair into some of those styles, but girl, let me tell you. I stank like a rabbit turd, and the hair flopped worse than a fat guy off a diving board."

"Say what?" Boom! Out there with the eff word. No one says that eff word.

"Oh yeah, honey, made a big splash for all the wrong reasons. My mom got me a crimper, and that changed my world." They ruffle their hair that's crinkle-cut waved. "No more flaxseed gel for me. I'll leave it to those pretty-boy bassists from your Londontown. Not everyone gets it, though. The look. The *vibe*."

"They should. Fashion is all about expressing who you are."

They stop with the preening and turn their full focus on me. "I *love* it. Expressing who you are. Love it." They look me over again. "Love those nails, girl. They don't allow long nails here at Pinedale, but those short ones are to die for. How'd you get those diamonds stuck on?"

"The salon."

Their brow creases. "That's some salon. You must

share their name with me."

"I got these done before we flew out. Maybe you can recommend a salon around here? They're due for a soak off."

"I just love your cute little English expressions. *Soak off*. But seriously, aren't you a little young to be in the seniors' bathroom?"

"Is there a rule? I didn't know. It's my first day."

"Don't sweat, honey. I won't tell if you won't." They go back to coloring in their lip lines. And add a beauty spot for good measure. "Most of the girls don't use this bathroom, though. They say it's haunted."

"Haunted?"

"Yeah, by losers and freaks." There's a solid sarcasm I can fully get behind.

"Ah, I see the school's inclusion policy is in full working mode," I retort.

"Inclusion policy? You've got a great sense of humor, you know that?" They extend a hand. "I'm Sam, by the way."

We shake, a peculiar gesture post-Covid and all, but in keeping with the retro vintage vibes, I guess.

"Lila B."

"What's the 'B' stand for?"

"Barely managing."

"First day treating you that well?"

I shrug. "It could be better. I did get one helluva welcome committee. There were these guys out front, leather jackets, lots of hair gel, plenty of bad attitude—"

"The Bruno Brothers. Yeah, there's a rumor about them. Can't say I've seen them myself, but I know all about their kind of nasty. Pushing people out the way, planting dead raccoons in lockers, pulling ponytails, that kind of childish shit. Exactly the type of crap they'd pull."

"Brothers?"

"Two of them. There's a third. They don't like anyone who's a little…different."

I wrap my arms around myself. " 'Stick to your own kind.' That's what one of them said to me."

"They spoke to you?" Sam's eyebrow arches again. "Now there's interesting."

"Right after they tripped up my buddy, Joe."

"At least you have a friend here."

I didn't correct them.

"My advice would be to stay out of their way. If you can. They don't much follow the rules."

"Good to know." We share a smile, and the day feels brighter. My first potential friend. "I better get to class before they send out a search warrant. Do you know where I can find class 2B? Or am I reading this wrong?"

"Aw, honey, I'm geographically challenged. I go by the colors. Red block, blue block, yellow block. Simple pimple."

"Got it. Thank you."

"Anytime. Stay cool."

Easy enough. One thing about Pinedale High, I'll need a sweater in the middle of a climate-change summer. A cute one with outsize sleeves or a ribbed bodice, but extra protection against this ancient building's chilliness.

A labyrinth of corridors greets me. Just one problem: All of the walls are painted off-white. All of the lockers are millennial grey. The floors are standard-issue cement.

There is no red block, blue block, yellow block. I

check my timetable again. Venue: Class 2B. In black type.

Second floor.

I set off in one direction and, mercifully, find the stairs. Maybe the color blocking is up there?

More off-white walls, more grey lockers.

What did Sam mean?

Simple pimple. Yeah. Right.

It's like I've been shoved into a tilt-a-whirl, and I can't find the way up.

I'll have to ask Joe.

If I can ever find him.

Chapter 6

What's for lunch?

So, that's a negative. I do not find Joe.

At eleven, the bell rings, and the place swarms with students.

Lunch.

I did not bring any lunch with me, but I have a few dollars my dad bounced me.

There was no cafeteria at my last school. There was a tuck shop where I could load up on sweets and chocolate. Don't ask me about the chocolate here, it's not worth a mention. Coffee, yes. Sandwiches, yes. Chocolate, hard pass.

I slip into a queue behind other students and play copycat to pretend I belong here.

Tray in hand, we shuffle forward inch by inch. See, I can do the imperial system!

It's an eclectic bunch, this Pinedale High. They sure have some style, though. There's a girl with pale-purple bell-bottom pants that are embroidered with daisies at the pockets. Her hair's in a headscarf, and I can see her falsies from here. There's a guy in what can only be described as gangsta chic but with a '90s flavor. And another rocking a solid '70s Afro, complete with a comb!

The Bruno Brothers must hate this place. *Everyone* seems different.

Still, they know how to find their classes and how to speak American.

It's almost my turn at the lunch counter. My palms start to sweat, and my heart talks to me through my ears. I can do this.

"Yeah? What'll it be kid?" The exhaustion of the woman behind the counter seeps through her stained polyester blouse and grey-rinsed apron.

"Chips, please." Behind me, someone groans, and I can sense their impatience beaming at me to move-the-hell-along.

"What? They're over there by the checkout. Next!"

"*Fries*. I'll have fries…and… *chicken fingers*. Oh, and tater tots. I've never had them before. It's exciting."

She doesn't acknowledge me at all, just slings the fried, deep fried, and even more deep fried onto my plate.

A voice low and menacing crowds my space. "I've been looking for you everywhere."

I nearly drop my tray.

It's the blond greaser from this morning. He's slick with that spicy-sweet smell, and it's clogging up my nostrils. His stare is intense, his eyes almost amber-colored, and his skin seems melted to the bones about his neck.

My knees buckle with fear. "Leave me alone," I hiss. I stride towards the checkout, aware of him cluttering up my peripheral vision.

"Hey, you don't have to be mean," calls out a girl's voice from behind me.

Yeah, you tell him, sister. There's no need to be mean. Accosting people in the lunch queue. And for what? *He* tripped Joe. Okay, his friend tripped Joe. That's their beef. Nothing to do with me.

A few seconds later, he's back at my side. "You don't understand. I need to talk with you."

My nerves are unravelling.

I go with my Plan B – ignore him.

His tone is insistent. "I said I need to talk with you, *capiche*?"

He's standing way too close. There's a gold cap on one of his front teeth. And his jeans are in the heaviest denim I've ever seen. Like there's no stretch in them. At all.

"*Capiche*? Who says that even?"

The guy in front of me turns to ogle the drama. His jaw is slack, and his glasses don't need tape to hold them together.

"Can you believe this guy?" I say, hoping he'll step in and chew Blondie here out.

He pushed his glasses farther up the bridge of his nose. "Are you talking to me?"

Before I can answer, the cashier calls him, and he scuttles forth.

I quickly follow, keen to get as much distance between me and this creep as possible.

Glasses boy turns on me. "Whoa, you can keep crazy on your side," he says, his hand upright in a *stop* gesture.

Crazy? There's a guy harassing me, and *he's* calling *me* crazy?

I bite my lip. My mother often said that there was no point arguing with a fool. They'd pull you down to their level, and soon, you wouldn't be able to tell who the fool was and who wasn't.

What was with this place?

A hand lands on my shoulder. I whip round in equal

parts horror and anger, spilling some of my tater tots and all of my good humor. "What the hell are you doing?"

Joe's face is a wave of emotions. Confusion, alarm, and then it's back to 100% pure pissed.

He takes a giant step back.

The red-hot burn of shame explodes through my cheeks. "I thought it was the other guy."

A quick glance reveals nothing but female students.

Blondie had vanished. Into the ether. Simply disappeared.

"But he was right there, that guy from this morning, you know, the ones with the leathers and the bad breath. The ones who—" I stopped from heaping a side serving of embarrassment onto Joe. He didn't need reminding of his concrete embrace.

"Hey, you're holding up the line."

With my head dropped low, I skulk to the cashier and pretty much throw money at her. I want the ground to swallow me up. I want to wave a magic wand and vanish. I'd even take an invisibility cloak.

Students are looking.

"You left your books in the lab. I picked them up for you." Joe's tone could refreeze the Arctic shelf.

They're in his hands and currently, I have no hands available.

"I got lost. I couldn't find the red and yellow and blue blocks." I can't find a place to sit either, every table is chocka with people while I'm here all nobby-no-mates.

"What are you talking about?"

"Ohmygod. The blocks. To find the classroom. Sam said that if I followed—"

"I don't know how they did things where you're

from, but we don't have red and yellow blocks. There's block one, block two, block three, got it? We're mostly in block two."

Why would Sam tell me to follow the colors? I thought we vibed. Maybe they *were* peeved that I was in the senior bathroom?

Nothing makes sense.

I spot a lone seat and make a beeline for it. Joe stacks my books on the edge of the table and splits.

Most of the tater tots I was so looking forward to are being crushed underfoot in the cafeteria line where I dropped them. My stomach is churning. There's still a whole lot of school day to get through, and so far, it's sucked.

What did that guy want with me? I've been in Pinedale all of two weeks. *Two weeks.* We've gone to the shops—the *stores*—we've gone to one of the parks, and I've spoken to no one at all but my father. This might be exaggeration, true. Yes, I said "hello" to the people working the tills, yes, I said "hi" to people out walking their dogs. No guys in leather jackets.

A bell rings. Are you kidding me? Lunch over already?

I stuff some chips—fries—into my mouth.

The janitor waiting to clean up the carnage left behind gives me a ghost of a wink.

Yeah, yeah, I'm heading out.

Chapter 7

The eye of the beholder

What constitutes a club? Ten people, thirty, a few hundred, thousands?

Three.

There are three students constituting the Photography Club. Plus me. But they have already been at great pains to explain that I'm not yet a member. I'm trying out. Auditioning.

Tomas sports a heavy camera round his neck like he's pregnant. Every now and then, he gives it a rub or a pat. "Lila, do you have a darkroom at home?"

"The back side of the house doesn't face the sun."

A pained expression. "You don't even know what a darkroom is. This is the Photography Club."

"But isn't that how I'll learn about what a darkroom is?"

To say we're in a shed is a compliment. It's worse than a shed. It's a tin can with a door. And then another door. Which Tomas then opens.

A single bulb swings from the ceiling, which he switches on.

All I can think of are interrogation scenes in hostage movies. Only there's no chair. There're washing lines and pegs, which is interesting as no one seems to hang out their washing here. They use the dryer. We use the sun.

On the tables are roasting pans all lined up.

"This is a darkroom. It's where we process our film. I assume you know what film is?"

Not a clue. "Sure."

Brian sniffs the air. "You do have an SLR, right?"

A what? "I've got two."

Zook jumps in. "What make?"

Uhhhmmmmmmm… "Only the best."

"Like mine? Top of the range." Tomas strokes his camera again, pointing the lens at me.

I bet he's fun at parties. A baby paparazzi sticking that thing in everyone's face.

"Only this one's a DSLR."

"I'm more interested in fashion photography. Ramps, runways, photo shoots, that kind of thing. Working with the stylists, the hair, the make-up, having and executing a vision."

The three of them look at me as if I've landed from Planet Girl.

"What kind of things do you shoot?" I'm thankful for the endless TV shows I've watched about fashion assistants and magazine goddesses. The lingo is lingoing. And it's giving me a veneer of confidence I don't feel.

"I'm interested in documentary mostly," says Zook. "I like to get to the honesty behind my subjects. Let the camera do the work and reveal the person inside. I'm not into the glitter or the photo editing—that's for vain celebrity types. Vacant, vacuous, meaningless. I want people to find meaning in my work. To question. To be moved. It's never just a picture. It's what's behind the picture."

There's a moment's silence.

I might need an antacid to digest that slice of word pie.

"Respect, man." Brian pats his fist to his heart and double-taps.

"How does the club work exactly?"

"We meet once a week and work on our monthly assignment," explains Tomas. "It's like a theme. This month, it's 'out of the ordinary', so it can be something like a fish out of water or an athlete holding a baby. What you don't see every day."

"I dibbed the woods, so you'll have to shoot somewhere else," says Brian. "This isn't a collab."

"And then do you exhibit?"

Tomas looks like he's choking on his own spit. "Do we exhibit? It takes years to reach the kind of dedication and pursuit of our craft that we're engaging in. It's an art. It *is* art. It's not about crass commercialism—"

"Or sharing it on the socials for the capitalist boys to scrape for their AI machines," adds Zook.

"Or shamelessly promoting products." Brian steeples his fingers together. "Do we exhibit? Like we'd stoop so low to brush with the great unwashed. Art is something that is transcendental. Spiritual even."

It certainly smells like spirits. Something sharp, almost vinegary. And a good deal of sweet men's body spray.

"So you're all documentary photographers then?"

All three nod.

I plead my case. "Fashion photography can be art. Fashion is art—"

"Consider, though, its primary purpose. It's to make money." Zook makes money sound filthy dirty.

I've always found money pretty helpful. Delightful even. You can buy stuff with it. Like shiny red lipgloss. Or doughnuts. Or music subscriptions.

Tomas's camera looks like it could feed a small family of five for a month.

"So what do you do with the pictures you shoot?" I had to ask. If no one was looking at it, did it even exist?

"Well, we discuss them," explained Brian. In s-l-o-w drawn-out style.

Duh? How could I be so dumb?

"The purpose is for us to critique with care, provide guidance on the craft. And then to delve into the meaning behind the visuals. To experience it."

You know, the girls' soccer team was starting to look more and more appealing. Take a ball and kick it into a net. That's it. Was it too late for me to switch to another club? One that was less, well, *adult*?

Tomas sighs. "I see you haven't brought your camera with you to today's session."

"I only started here today. I didn't know that I'd be here."

He shrugs. "I'll loan you one of mine. I assume you know how to change the lens?"

"It might be a different make."

"Perhaps you can shoot around the buildings. There's some great architecture that can frame your shots. The school dates back to before the '50s, you know." He hands me a camera.

My first time. If I want to take a photo, I point my phone and click. It even has filters. And you can share it with your friends immediately. Did they know that?

Tomas sounds like a future university professor. "You change the shutter speed here. Adjust the aperture there. And yeah, don't drop it. We'll develop next week. Oh yes, that's a 24 film. So plan, then click. No one wants to waste their film, got it?"

There will be a lot of searching online the second these guys disappear to be at one with their art. Shutter speed? Aperture? 24 film?

There's a silence that stretches into next year.

"Oh, shall I go now?"

"Your subjects await," says Brian. All three want the space to clear so they can gossip about me and my utter uselessness.

I can hear it now.

This girl who doesn't even know what a darkroom is wants to fight for a place in here, this shed of greatness.

This girl who wants to be a fashion photographer? Can you imagine? What sort of banality is that? Clothes? Like my heavy metal T-shirt of a band I've never heard in my life.

This girl who thinks money is a good thing. What good is money? It's only the stuff you buy food, shelter, clothing, and dark rooms with?

Still. Tomas gave me his camera. Can't hurt to take a few pics. As soon as I find out how to.

Chapter 8

Home sweet home

The key to the front door hides in a plant pot.

I fish it out. It's a habit that I'm sure will fade away with time. Dad says plenty of people keep their homes unlocked.

We've nothing to steal anyway. Anything of real value's long gone.

Unopened boxes cram the hallway. Some have "fragile" written on the side. Would it help if humans did the same?

I can't get used to this house.

There's so much…space. We have a separate room for our washing machine. *Its own room.* There's also a basement that I can't wrap my head around. Why do we need a basement? I don't like to go down there. It's damp, cold, and smells of mushrooms. I bet there's a toad.

The house is also quiet.

As if no one lives here. There's no TV or someone smacking dishes in the kitchen or even the hoover.

Almost eerie quiet. Sometimes I say something out loud, like "boo" or "blah", to hear anything other than my own breathing.

I charge up the stairs to my room, which has knobbly wood floors and overlooks a giant apple tree.

My last bedroom, I could look out into lots of other people's windows in the building behind us.

One day, I'll stop comparing everything. It does no good to compare.

Tell that to my mind that drifts any chance it gets to everything I miss about home, my real home, my former home. The sleety gray sky, the kebab shops, my friends. Let's not talk about my friends. Long-distance doesn't work, does it?

Jo and I promised to keep in touch, but there's a time difference.

Virtual conversations aren't the same as heading to charity shops to rummage through their new hauls or lounging about in Jo's room talking crap about nothing at all.

The bitter bite of loneliness sinks deep. I wait for the feeling to pass. It's not always bad, that heave of emotion. Other times, it stops me in my tracks.

I change out of my outfit and switch into a pale-pink onesie. It used to belong to my mom. During her "lucid" moments.

My homework list is alarmingly long. Who does that to someone on their first day? I have to catch up on all the work I've missed in Biology, I'm ahead in Math, I have to read *Wuthering Heights*, and I need to hustle my way through a whole new language.

But lunch was such a non-starter, and my stomach is now so empty it could eat itself.

A feint mew ruffles the silence.

Wait.

And there it is again.

I wrestle with my window, which eventually opens.

The mewing is louder now.

Despite repeat scanning, I can't identify the culprit.

I head back downstairs and out into the garden, under the tree. The mewing ramps up as I step forward.

A tiny black kitten, almost a shadow, balances on one of the branches. One look at me, and it retreats farther up, its mewing loud and constant.

"C'mon, little kitty." I whisper, cajole, call, tweet, whistle, you name it.

Kitty remains steadfast.

I try another tactic and return with a can of tuna.

Kitty gives up the fight and wobbles to where I can comfortably scoop her up. She about fits in my palm, one eye weeping, her little ribcage visible under her scrawny fur. Her paper-thin claws swipe at me, digging deep and painfully so.

"Alright, alright, you can have some treatskie. Let's get you inside." I say it as though it has a choice.

Moments later, the kitten's face is burrowed in the tuna, emitting happy growls with every bite.

"And where did you come from?" It's less weird to talk out loud when you're talking to an animal. You're still talking to yourself, but it feels like you're not. Because there's the kitten. Who, you never know, might respond. Unlikely. But never say never.

"Is your mommy looking for you? I bet she's worried."

There's no milk. Our fridge contains almost exclusively beer. That's the only thing that seems to keep my father going these days. Come home, get drunk, pass out, go back out to work. He's been like this ever since, well, ever since my mom died.

He blames himself.

He doesn't say that.

But I know he does.

Part of me blames him too.

It's a tiny part though, and I keep it well hidden. Sometimes, when he's really drunk, he's scary.

"Dinner won't make itself, will it now, kitty?" Distraction is easy with this one. Their eyes are round, yellow, and so, so cute. "Shall we have cereal without the milk or cheese on toast? If we scrape off the mold?"

I'm kidding. We don't have any cereal.

There's a frozen lasagna. I switch on the oven. It says you're supposed to microwave it, but the microwave is also in the crate across the Atlantic, so the oven it will have to be.

"We're going to have to look for your mummy."

I've heard the theories of the cat distribution system, but kittens do not randomly appear. There's either a mother cat close by, a kid wondering where his kitty got to, or some mean jerk who's dumped them.

Jo's cat went missing for three months after their geyser blew and she got caught in the plumber's van and was moved ten blocks away. Another kid found Pookey—that was the cat's name— and claimed her, citing the cat distribution system. But Jo was out of her mind with worry. They eventually got her back, but that other kid thought it was theirs. Legit thought it was theirs.

I believe there was a bit of a skirmish.

Facts are facts, though.

There's always a rational explanation.

It's cool to think there're kitties falling out of the sky like four-legged, fluffy, magical gifts, but that's not what's happening.

There's no such thing.

Even my mom, who thought she saw...*things*, didn't believe in the cat distribution system.

She *did* believe that cats could see through the veil to the next world. Hmmm.

This kitty is very cute though. And persistent.

I'll go next door and ask around. This kitty's owner must be mad with panic over where their gorgeous-worgeous-borgeous itty-bitty-kitty is.

It curls up on the counter and watches me whip up the gourmet delight of frozen lasagna, eat a quarter, put the rest on a plate in the fridge for my dad, then do the washing up.

He works late a lot. He says they're working on some major acquistion, I don't know.

I don't think he likes coming home.

She's not here.

I get it, I do.

It's the little things that trip me up. The chocolate-and-peanut bars in the cupboard because she knew they were my favorite. The evenings we'd watch her reruns of vampire TV shows and argue over who had more rizz in the love triangle between the brothers and their human love interest. The smell of her clothes.

There's no rhythm or rhyme anymore.

No routine.

No sense of the familiar.

My father drifts further and further away on his sea of beer cans.

If I'm busy being busy, I don't have to think about it too much.

I sweep the kitchen floor and wipe down the rest of the countertops. I leave the porch and the hallway light on and head up to my bedroom. With the kitty.

Today was… a *lot.*
Tomorrow will be a better day.
Won't it?
An uncomfortable feeling digs at me.
It will be better.
Maybe.

Chapter 9

Dreams can't hurt you

I'm on a bike pedaling with a blind fury I didn't know was possible.

It's dusk, the sun's setting, and I'm in the—

The woods.

I've veered off the track. The bike bounces and bends over the rocks and the needles. It squeaks, and the spokes hum.

The air is spearmint cold.

My lungs burn with panic.

My calves tense with fear.

Behind me, someone follows. No, *tracks* me.

I had a head start. A whole four minutes. It's shortening with each second, and the gap toward my escaping widens.

They're in a car, one of those ones with the top that folds down. White, sleek, and expensive. A gang of students. Good-looking, popular, and spoiled.

Drunk.

Dangerous.

And gaining.

The bike's not designed for off-road. It was a present. From my dad before he left. A shiny red racer with a bright-silver bell. For ambling through the suburbs, the wind in my hair, the open road an invitation.

He never saw me ride my bike. Look at me now, Dad! I sure am riding, I'm riding so fast, you'd be so proud of me. So proud.

I'm dreaming. This is a dream.

Every pedal push is like punching through brick. A muscle pulls taut in my thigh, but I keep pushing forward.

The bike falters, and I bite my tongue hard. Stinging pain and salty blood swirl in my mouth. It brings me up short.

This is real. This is happening.

It's happening right now.

Adrenaline's driving the show.

My heart thunders in my ears.

I can barely breathe.

They sound their horn. The car revs and scratches over the gravel paths. Skipping dust. And they're yelling, calling, shouting. Names. They're calling me something, but I can't make it out. I don't want to make it out.

I've heard it all before. So many times.

Sticks and stones break bones.

But words kill. Slow poison suffocation.

My padlock chain smacks, duff, duff, duff with every pedal. On my wrist is the pink ribbon my mother gave me. For when I have the jitters. I can hear her, soft, pink, warm. *It's to focus you back on the here and now when you have the jitters.* That's what she calls my nerves. The jitters.

I can't reach it.

It's tied with a loose knot, and it slips farther with each bump.

My sweaty palms slide on the handlebars.

Get a grip. Keep it together.

I can't pedal fast enough.

My lungs burn so bad I want to vomit.

I don't know where the hell I am. Where I'm going. A kid went missing in here a year ago. They never found his body. There's a rumor about a cave. Coyotes. Bears. Bigfoot.

The animals hounding me are the regular human kind.

Popular. So popular. There's always passion for blood sports.

It's getting darker, darker, darker. Any second now, the sun will poof. And vanish.

I will not be like that kid.

A voice climbs into my head—not mine.

I could outrun them. If I dump this bike, I could duck behind a tree, hide somewhere. Wait it out.

Something's tugging at the wheels, tripping up my progress. Slowing me down.

The pom-poms on my socks, they're catching in the spokes.

Those headlights spotlight me. They're gaining, Jesus, they're gaining.

"Get him." Crystal clear this time.

They're that close.

A warrior cry rings out. Vicious. Feral.

Out for blood. My blood.

I duck out of the light into where the woods are thicker. The sun's fading fast.

No one will find me, rushes through my thoughts. *My mom won't find me.* Just like that kid. They'll search and search. Everyone will talk about me for a few weeks. Then they'll forget.

And I'll be forever lost in the woods. Trying to find

my way back.

The handlebars turn one way, my back wheels another. I almost skid the bike to a stop. Almost.

Faster, you have to be faster.

Push. Goddammit. Push.

The dirt here's less like gravel, more like creeping thick vegetation. The wheels struggle to get purchase. It's quiet, so quiet.

This can't be how it happens. It can't.

The emotion chokeholds me. A sheer naked terror.

Confusion distracts me. But that's not *my* voice.

It's someone else's.

Someone else's thoughts.

I'm not racing through a forest.

They are. This is theirs. Not mine.

The woods close in, close up. The car's engine is less insistent. I want to turn around. Don't turn around. Keep going.

If you turn around, you'll slow down, and they'll catch you. And when they catch you, what do you think they'll do?

You heard what they called you.

Don't stop moving until you're out of these woods.

You never get out of these woods.

The back of my neck is icy cold with truth.

I'm getting out of these woods. Joe. What's he doing here?

You're dreaming, remember?

I claw and gasp to catch my breath that's running ahead of me.

The bike topples forward. I head straight down a slope; my breath catches and lodges at the back of my throat. The bike gathers equal momentum and speed.

There's no stopping.

I jam my heels back on the pedals. Hard. Slow down there, slow down. My hands pump on the brakes.

The bike hits something. Time slows all the way down. The back wheel lifts up, up, up and over. Tips me out. I'm falling forward, but—

One second, I held tight and now…

I've let go.

All of me has let go. A complete surrender.

I'm flying.

Higher and higher into the air.

A slow-motion catapult that brings me face-to-face with a fear I can't control. My stomach sinks to a new watery liquid depth, a bottomless ravine of infinite terror.

And I can't control it.

I'm falling. Faster and faster.

Inevitable. Powerless.

I land hard. My head strikes something thick, hard, unmoving.

There's darkness for a second. But there's no pain.

I feel for the ribbon, my pink ribbon. It's always on my right wrist. I promised my mother I'd always wear it. I pretended like it meant nothing.

It's everything.

It's a line from me to her, a comfort. A reassurance that whenever anything awful happens, she's always there.

The love is always there.

My wrist tingles where it's bent backwards. It's wet, sticky even.

There's no ribbon.

It's gone.

I can't hear them anymore.

I can't hear anything.

I wake with a rush of movement.

I climb out of bed, slam on the light, walk to the window and open it before I fully come to consciousness.

Sam.

The dream was about Sam.

Chapter 10

Morning coffee

My phone reads 6:01.
My brain hurts.
My body aches.
Next to me, the kitten sleeps like the dead.
There's nothing like broken sleep to fog your brain and fill your eyes with dryness.
There are dreams. And then there's whatever *that* was.
Dreams are slippery things.
Mostly, they're a random rehash of memories and thoughts and stuff I've looked at during the day. They also have that strange retroactive thing where you can suddenly remember an event and then question, was that really real or was that part of a dream I'm remembering?
Dreams are unreliable.
I've been in a circus, spoken to dragons, and flown over cities at night. Shown up for exams naked, had a brother and a sister, and visited a Paris that looked more like Birmingham.
I've also had those dreams where my mom is still alive. And then the awful moment between dream and awake when I remember she's not.
My worst nightmare.
But last night's dream...it felt real.

Not imagined, dredged up from my subconscious.

Real. Like it was happening right now.

Like it was happening to me.

As if I saw the whole thing through Sam's eyes.

An out-of-body, in-body experience.

An anxiety buzzes through me like I've had too much caffeine. My heart's revving, and my fingers twitch like fireflies.

It's dread.

It can't be real. Obvs.

A dream is your brain hallucinating.

I pick up my phone again.

Doomscroll through the toc app. Search again for Sam. They must be on the socials somewhere. Who's not on social media? Especially someone with that kind of passion for fashion? I bet they have a whole '80s-influencer thing going.

I open and close the photo app, scroll through without seeing.

It's a dream.

Only a dream.

Sam is probably putting together today's banging outfit and sculpting their cheeks with the three different colors of blush like they had yesterday. No contour, no highlight. Only those three shades of pink. Proper old school.

And a bike? Sam? On a bike? I can't picture it.

And boom! I'm back in the dream, pedaling, pushing, a fear choking me in its stranglehold.

Not real.

I must've seen it in a movie.

There's a detail I can't remember. It seems important. Only that part of the dream hazes and phases, blanking out completely. Don't you hate it when it does that? It's right there, you remember it, and…whoosh…it sinks without a trace.

It's now 6:05.

A whole four minutes gone.

I get up, go pee, and head downstairs to the kitchen. The kitten follows me, a miniature shadow at my feet.

I shove a pod into the coffee machine and wait. Cats are not supposed to drink milk. But kittens? Especially one this small?

There's movement from the lounge, or what will be the lounge when all our furniture arrives. All of my senses rush to the present second.

The hallway light is still on.

There's nothing to grab. The knives are in their box marked "Kitchen".

My phone's upstairs. But who do I call? What's the police number here?

A second later, my heart somersaults into my mouth before crash-landing in the pit of my stomach. "Dad."

He's in yesterday's clothes. Crumpled, thick stubble, hair askew.

My mood switches to a different kind of anxiety. He must have passed out on that old recliner the house donated to us. My gaze switches to the fridge—did he eat anything? Or did he scrape it into the bin? How many beer cans surround the recliner? One? Two? Ten?

"Morning, Lila." His finger points at the kitten who's weaving about my feet. "What's that?"

Grumpy. A bear with a hangover.

"I'm going to ask around, see who she belongs to. I found her in the tree. It was too late to go door-to-door, but I'll do it today. Don't worry, I put together a litter tray with soil from out the garden. In my room."

"The laundry room might be a better spot."

The coffee machine spits its last drop. I hand the cup to him. "Here you go. Tough day yesterday?"

He doesn't answer. More of a grunt, if anything. No milk in his coffee either. Black and strong.

He didn't used to be like this.

One day, the old dad will return. One day.

I give the kitten some milk in a saucer and the rest of the tuna. It takes one bite and then turns up its nose. Such a kitty. Now it's squawking for something else. Salmon, maybe? Caviar? A big juicy steak?

Dad drains his coffee and slides another pod into the machine. "I'm sure there's an SPCA or shelter you can take it to."

So no chance of keeping it. A grey cloud funks my mood. Not that I wanted to keep it. Anyway, I'm sure it belongs to someone else.

"I'll try the neighbors first, and then I'll go there."

He nods. "Good."

Case closed then. Is it wrong I feel the teeniest bit of disappointment?

It's purring now like it's swallowed a tractor into its belly. One happy little kitty.

Dad picks up his second coffee. "Gotta get ready for work. I might be late this evening…presentation…you know." He pauses. "Oh, and good luck for your first day today. It is today, isn't it? You'll be fine. It's a great place. I should know. Still got my yearbook." He smiles with a faraway look. For a moment, he resembles the dad I knew. "You'll knock it out of the park, I'm sure of that. Look how popular you were at your last school. You'll have a whole new bunch of friends in no time."

I don't have the heart to tell him that I've already lived a perfectly awful first day.

He finishes his second coffee with one gulp. "And don't believe the stories. There's no such thing as ghosts, right?" There's an edge to his voice. Scary Dad is back in play. The one who announced we were leaving, out of the blue, and wrapped up our house and shoved us onto a plane to the middle of nowhere.

Being around this dad is like trying not to make a noise walking on dead leaves.

My voice rises an octave. "Ghosts? Absolutely not. Mom just liked to…she had a vivid imagination."

"And you know what happened to her." It's a warning. "That stuff doesn't exist. It… messes with people's heads. I don't want to hear any of that stuff from you."

Last night's dream is screaming at me with big blazing neon lights, "Look at me! Look at me!"

"Every school that's been standing for decades has its own folklore, and Pinedale High's no different."

The kitten digs its claws into my calf and mountaineers up my leg.

Every grab is a sharp stab of pain. I scoop it up, and it nestles in my hand. "It'll be all good, Dad."

"Just remember what I said."

"I will."

"You'll kill it." He winks at me and heads upstairs.

Chapter 11

Sometimes they come back

Sam's circling my mind.
Are they okay?
Do they have a bike?
Who were those guys?
Are they okay?
I've tried ignoring the thoughts, but they return with alarming force. It's like trying to not think of a pink polar bear. You're thinking of a pink polar bear now, aren't you?

My feet cannot carry me any faster, even if I swing my hips and butt like someone shoved a poker up there. The school's less than a block away. There's the main gate with a drib drab of late students. And then there's me, burning lungs and blistering feet marching to make it mostly on time.

We live close enough to the school to walk. Right now, I wish we backed on the place. Less distance to cover.

The clock will not be in my favor. Yes, it's my fault. No, I don't have time blindness.

I put the kitty back on my bed, rested for a second…and dozed off.

It happens to all of us.

Forget any semblance of vintage chic dressing. I

slung a jacket over my pj top and hitched up some old jeans. Sneakers. Without socks. There's no make-up, no accessories, not a thing.

Because I know who'll be waiting for me at the top of those stairs.

Oh, and there he is now. All fire-breathing and smoldering with resentment.

My buddy, Joe.

The one lens of his tape-repaired glasses slopes down. He's checking out the time on his phone, carrying a stack of books under one arm. Multi-accomplished.

I stretch up the stairs, two at a time. "There was a huge pile up on the mega freeway. You should see it."

Ah, once upon a time, there were people who laughed at my silly jokes. His face doesn't move. He's in a jacket with lettering on it.

"Just like in the movies," I say out loud. Because, to be honest, I have never seen a letter jacket, if that's what you call it, in real life. So much of my childhood has been spent looking at the sets of America, and now, I'm here. And there's a weird familiarity to it. Like the school buses. Or shopping malls. Or diners.

I've seen it all before, and yet, I know nothing.

"Are you for real?" he responds.

"Only on Saturdays."

He cuts with the pleasantries. Always to the point. Straight down to business. "Hurry, we might make it."

We nearly do, too.

First-period mathematics class, our target, speed, our middle name.

We swing round one corner, hurtle down the next, and then…well, THEN—

There they are.

The Bruno Brothers.

My heart catapults out of my mouth.

Same black leather jackets, superior-quality denim, and shitkicker army boots. Blondie's whole face opens up at the sight of us. Curious. The other two? Happy to see us but with an unpleasant deadness in their eyes. Like the eyes of a great white shark before it sinks its teeth in and r-i-p-s. Quick PSA: Don't watch shark movies. Those dead eyes follow you forever. I mean, for-ever.

My feet slide over the well-worn floors as I peddle backward. "No, no, no."

Yes, yes, yes.

It happens so quickly I'm sure I imagined it.

The smoker jerk who brayed in my face yesterday about "my kind" scoops past Joe, making as if to pass him. Casual-like. Then swings his fist under Joe's stack of books. Pow! Sends them flying like confetti pushed out of one of those tube things.

To be fair, Joe's instincts kick in quick. He grasps and stumbles to catch the books. Too late. A series of thuds as the books crash land, bent spines and splayed pages.

An outraged fury beats out of my mouth before I can corral it back. "What the hell is wrong with you? First, yesterday and now...*this.*"

I love how words completely fail me when I need them most.

The other brother, not Blondie, cackles and guffaws. He reminds me of Jo's younger brother, who'd do stupid shit like dancing in front of the TV screen during our favorite show.

"It's not funny," I say. "Genuinely, what the hell is wrong with you?"

I can ask the same question of Joe, who is practicing ignorance with an overly controlled, icy calm. One by one, he's picking up his books, smoothing them back into place and gathering them up.

I can't keep it in. "Seriously, you're not going to say anything?"

Cackle boy brushes past me accidentally on purpose. "Don't go cruisin' for a bruisin', Daddy-O".

Just like something my grandfather would have said.

These guys are pathetic.

Blondie's gaze is delivering a big ole heap of unsettling. What do these guys want from me? Is it Joe? Is there a beef there? *What?*

Ah, but I'm also forgetting that for some guys, this is fun. They do it because they can. They do it because no one stops them. It's sport. A mild amusement. Something to keep them entertained.

Clearly, they've had this morning's fun because they walk away from the scene of the crime.

Maybe Joe's right to ignore them.

Childish pranks. That's what Sam had said.

It dawns on me that in my dream there was another group of asshats. Was this place a breeding ground for total jerks? Or were these the same ones? If there was any truth in the dream. Which there wasn't. Because it was a dream.

Only sometimes, dreams did turn out to be true. Like that time I dreamed what I'd get for my eleventh birthday, or where Jo could find her lost roller skates—bathroom, Clapham Junction; or when my teacher was pregnant—she seemed like two people instead of one, and that was before there was a bump.

I pick up a book that managed to turn a few

somersaults before landing near a rubbish bin—*trash can*. "This one seems okay. *Advanced Trigonometry*. Sounds exciting. Loan it to me when you're done."

Joe snatches it from me and adjusts his wobbly frames. "What is your problem?"

"*My* problem?"

"Yes, your—you know what? Forget it. I don't have time for this."

He marches off, pure sulk and strop.

Ah, so today will be more of the same. Good to know. It's like walking into an upside-down house, and everyone's correcting me that it's the right way up.

Well, it isn't.

Joe can choose to ignore those guys. Fine. His choice.

I can be angry at their behavior. Fine. My choice.

But *what's my problem?*

To me?

And not *those* guys?

That's, well…nuts.

I gather myself together, straighten my popular sci-fi baby pj top, and make to follow Joe. We're properly late now. Will this end up being my first detention? Or will I be made to stand outside the class? They did that with disruptive students at my primary school.

A strange sensation floods over my back and creeps up to my neck. It's cold; it's invasive. An intense case of the chills. My breath catches in my throat.

You know how you know when someone's watching you? That's the feeling.

It's that Blondie. I'm sure of it.

He almost seemed *happy* to see me. But that's ridiculous. Of course, he was happy to see me. Someone new to pick on.

When I pick up enough courage to look back, no one's there.

Chapter 12

Into the thick of it

I can't find Sam. As they're a senior, I don't have anyone to ask about their whereabouts either.

They're pretty distinctive though. I reckon I'd see them, head and shoulders and high hair above the rest.

Joe's not talking to me.

He sits next to me in my classes and stares pointedly the other way, giving me a view of his chiseled, jaw-clenched profile. Like a rock.

Speaking of which, he did text me.

—*We've got a rendezvous in the woods.*—

There's a pretty redhead who sits a few down from us in History who has a huge thumping crush on Joe.

She checks him out every few seconds like he might have moved state or something while her focus was elsewhere. When she's not texting under the desk, a Pinedale special skill, she's twirling her pen around her notebook, probably writing his name.

Yes, I made that up. I bet she'd kill for him to be texting her.

—*Football field. 3pm. Don't be late. Bring ur stool bags.*—

He does mean soil, right? Visions of poo bags abound. We used to tie the poo bag to Jo's dog whenever we took Trixie—the dog—for a trot. Two bags. One to protect the hand and scoop. The other to dispose of said poo. Or poop. Same shit, different way.

In this morning's flurry, I forgot the stool bags in the kitchen.

I can't say I have any spares on me either. You know, for emergencies.

The redhead catches me watching her and flushes pinker than a shrimp.

When class is dismissed, I make a beeline for her. "Hey. Hi. So, Joe's my partner for the aquarium project, and he's left his soil bags at home."

She can't help it. Her eyes search him out at the mere mention of his godly name.

"He'd love to ask you, but you know guys, they're...stupid. Do you have some you could loan us?"

She flickers back to the here and now, momentarily adrift in her Joe fantasies. "For Joe? He asked?"

"Not in as many words, but yes."

"Sure. How many do you need?"

"I don't know. He's big into the environment, so I'd imagine none, seeing as they're plastic and all, but as he's big into the environment, many, so he can take more stool samples than anyone else."

Her face crinkles. "That's how many?"

"Four or five?"

She hands me an entire box. "Take what you want. You're lucky to have Joe as your buddy. He's a legend. And a good guy too."

"Pretty sure he has his off days."

"He's always upbeat, peppy, the first with an encouraging word."

"Is that so?" I yank out a wedge of bags. "Thank you. We'll pick up half the forest with these."

There're still a few minutes to go before 3 PM. I follow the blocks to try to find the seniors' bathroom. I haven't had success yet. All the buildings look the same. And contrary to Tomas, Brian, and Zook's theory, there wasn't much to be gleaned from the space as an art subject either.

My 24 photos will reveal long shadows and the floor. Turns out, old cameras can't take as many photos as you'd like, and you can't see what you've shot either. That joy is reserved for our next club meeting.

I don't know why I think I'll find Sam in the seniors' bathroom other than that's where I found them the last time.

They weren't in the cafeteria.

They weren't near the lockers.

They weren't in the hallway.

Are they in a ditch somewhere because their bike hit a rock while some bullies chased them through the woods at night?

I shake off the unease that's in my bones.

Just a dream. Only a dream.

Time to meet Joe for our field trip.

Now, the football field—the lower football field because it's the one that backs onto the woods—should be easy to find.

Follow the woods.

Aha!

Joe's a small dot on the other side of the pitch. They're having practice, so I can't walk through it. There's also a team of cheerleaders tearing up the field. I've never seen cheerleaders in my life. Only on TV. The redhead's one of them. She's throwing her stick in the air. Impressive.

I walk the perimeter of the fields toward Joe.

My phone says 2:58. I'm not late, I'm early. A whole two minutes early.

"Did you bring the bags?"

I pull them triumphantly from my pocket. "Ta-da!"

"Are those the biodegradable kind?"

"Er, no. I borrowed them from someone else."

I'm waiting for the upbeat, peppy guy to say something enthusiastic, like, we'll make it work. Or they're being used to create a whole new aquarium.

"You should check. We're breathing in microplastics all the time. It's terrifying."

"I agree. I couldn't agree more."

He gives me an odd look.

Oh, he thinks I'm joking. Have I ever met anyone who understands me less? I change the subject. "Where were you thinking of starting? I'm assuming you're familiar with these trees?"

He jumps straight into serious environmentalist mode. "The far south side of the woods has the most-dense vegetation, so I figured there. Unless you had another idea?"

"Happy to go with the south side."

"It's a twenty-minute walk."

"Okay."

"Just saying."

"I can manage a twenty-minute walk." That's the distance from the underground to my mom's favorite movies. Movies were her thing. We used to go every Friday afternoon. Our thing. "We walk a lot back home."

He moves with long strides. "Let's go then."

You can still see through the trees here. There's even a path. I eye the vegetation with some trepidation.

"Are there stinging nettles? My Nan had stinging nettles in the fields by her house."

"No. No poison ivy either."

"What's that?"

"Similar kind of thing. Don't get it on your skin. Stings."

"Is there a road through here?"

"Yeah, on the other side. Through one section. There used to be a picnic area. But then some kid got lost, and they closed the trails round there."

"Was that the one whose body was found in the cave?"

"Where did you hear that?" There's utter disbelief in his voice.

Oh, I remember. My dream.

He turns into a more wooded area, off the path. "This kid's body was never found. It was like thirty years ago or so."

"My mistake."

"There're no caves in these woods. Someone would've found them already." There's such confidence in his words.

But that dream.

Just a dream, Lila, it was just a dream.

Chapter 13

Common ground

Joe wasn't kidding about the south side of the forest.

The canopy completely covers the sky. Sure, it's day outside, and the sun is beaming, but in here, it's so shaded it may as well be night.

He also wasn't exaggerating about the undergrowth. I had to hike.

Climb over dead trees, mountaineer over rocks, and there's even a tiny stream.

Pretty sure it was longer than twenty minutes, too.

"And you're positive you know how to get us back out again?"

He doesn't look up from his biology experiment. "Will it feel better if you ask me a fourth or fifth time?"

Joe is holding forth on why we have to be in the deeper darker parts of the wood because that's where all the good fungi live.

I wish he was more of a "fun guy". He might look like a jock, but he's all kinds of book smart. Still, watching him scrape and jar is kind of therapeutic.

"There are strange noises in here." There were. Birds I don't recognize. Not that I can identify anything other than a crow. "This isn't a bear type of woods, is it?"

"Yes."

"Are you serious?"

"Don't you have bears in your woods?"

"No. Our woods are more like...we have foxes."

Joe's gloved hands burrow under a pile of leaves, and he uses some metal instrument to scrape the ground. "Pass me that bag, please."

I pass. Like a surgeon's apprentice. It seems a high-tech project for us lowly students.

"Mr. Rourke's instructions weren't this intense. It's a chance to try out some of this stuff I've saved up for. I'm curious about what's in the soil, water, that kind of thing."

It was as if he read my mind.

Joe has his jars and tools set out meticulously. "What's London like?"

"Loud, fast, modern. I miss the city part." My ass rests on a pile of dirt. Ants bite my ankles. And there are bears in here. "I miss being able to get around. I could go on the tube and visit my friend. Or we'd take the bus. There was so much to see. Our school was very different too. We had a uniform, and there were lots of rules."

"Why'd you move here? Seems like a very different vibe."

"My father grew up near here. He went to Pinedale, can you believe it? He got a job opportunity he couldn't refuse, so we packed up, and here we are." It's almost the truth.

Joe hands me a jar. "Your turn."

I copy him, careful to find a particularly rich-looking specimen filled with dead material. Apparently, that's where all the magic is. I hold up my jar. "What do you think? Good job?"

"Great job." He sounds surprised. "You can take

that area there. And I'll work over by that tree."

We fall into a comfortable routine—scraping, packing, and marking our soil specimens. It's way, way over the top for this project—and if it isn't, I'm in serious trouble; this is way too hardcore.

"How are you finding it here in Pinedale?"

I take my time to answer. "It's hard. Everything is so different. I'm sure I'll get used to it, though."

There's actual dirt under my fingernails, and somehow, I'm having an okay time.

"Don't mix your samples."

I was *almost* having an okay time.

"Sorry, you're doing a great job. I didn't mean to…"

"My dad's the same. When he's working. It has to be right. Perfect, even. We always used to tease him that he needed to loosen up, have fun, seize the moment!"

"We?"

"Oh, my mom and I." A lump takes that moment to lodge in my throat. "Anyhoo. What's with the Bruno brothers? Why are they so mean?"

If ever there were a time to ask, it is now. He could always march away and leave me in the forest. Only that wouldn't look so great on his record. Straight A student, athlete, and sadist.

He looks confused, then his face brightens. "The Brunos? You mean the guys who write *Weirder Times*?"

Ooooh, that's where I'd heard that name before. "Oh yeah, no, not them, the ones at school."

"Don't know them. But yeah, *Weirder Times* is my absolute all-time favorite show."

Well, whaddaya know? "Mine too."

For the first time since our less-than-auspicious meeting, I catch a glimpse of the Joe others seem to know. His whole face is aglow, his eyes shining, and his body relaxed. "For real? I hate how we have to wait another whole year for the next season to drop. That's three years since the last one."

"Right? They'll be in a retirement home by the time we get to season five."

"Which one's your favorite?"

"Season two, so far. Season four was mid. Though I do have to say, the scenes with Charlie when they have to get her out of the—

"The Topsy-Turvy? 100% pure power, right there. And with the music? But yeah, season four *B* was more fan-service than anything else. Season four *A* was great."

"Right? I get gooseflesh thinking about it. I hope they don't kill Charlie off. I didn't love her in season two, but she's my favorite favorite, except for Pete."

"Everyone's beloved babysitter."

"Goes without saying."

He warms to his theme. "You're not a fan of Carrie?"

"Fifty-fifty. She started off great, but then it got lost around that whole superhero arc. Psychics are not my best trope in a series. It's so convenient. All Professor Y-style, put my hand to my head and read the future. Then, they change their mind about how it works. And how it must be the best superpower ever, but the reality is you sound psycho. I liked Carrie and Charlie in season three, though, before everything got played out."

That might've been the most I've spoken to anyone aloud in days. Weeks, even. And to *Joe*. I never would have seen that coming.

"I can get behind that. I hope they stick the landing."

"You and about one hundred million fans."

It's like a whole new Joe. "That many?"

"Most-streamed show ever. It's big back home too. I binged the first three in time for season four *A*. I get the hype."

"Yeah, for sure" He's totally relaxed now, even in his pharmaceutical gloves covered with soil. "Let's finish up here before it gets dark. Don't want to meet a Gogron from the Topsy-Turvy."

"Please, no." I shudder. "But there are bears…"

"Bears… you stay out of their way, they'll stay out of yours, now a Gogron… you're not so lucky…"

We gather up our soil samples, a different shape in the space between us forming. Maybe he could be my buddy, Joe.

Stranger things have happened.

I broach THE question again. "So, there's no Bruno brothers in the school?"

"Not that I know of." There's nothing about his tone or expression to suggest he's lying. No bluffing to save face. Nothing like that.

Maybe Sam had their name wrong. The Bruno Brothers. Of course, it's the same name of the legendary writer/director brothers. Why hadn't I noticed that earlier? I even follow them on the toc.

I dare not ask Joe a third time.

Not so soon after we seem to have found common ground.

Chapter 14

True Blue

It is proper dark when I finally get home.
Dad isn't there.
The kitten is.
Hungry. Squawking. And beyond adorable.
I'll check with the neighbors, I will. It seems rude to bust in on them during dinner, asking questions about kittens. Disturbing their family time, their TV time, their catching up on their taxes time.
"Hey, Fuzzwhat, what if your owner is looking for you? Knocking on this door and you're on the other side, only no one's home to answer."
Like me talking to the kitten, somehow expecting an answer.
Fuzzwhat—have to call it something and not a proper name either. It can be a ridiculous nonsense of a name because I can't keep them, so Fuzzwhat it is—inhales their breakfast tuna and milk.
Dad did not come home last night.
My phone shows no new messages.
It's not even as if he popped in for a change of clothes and then ducked out again. He's just...not here.
The move was supposed to make things better, not worse.
My heart sinks, but I pump it back up again.

His work is very intensive. I don't know what he does exactly, but it's to do with buying up companies that are struggling and then bringing in new investors to help give them the boost they need. It's all about figures, rows and rows of figures, and poring over graphs, and juicy thick research documents that outline how a company works. It's called a prospectus. I guess it's like mining for business gold.

He calls it research.

It's how we could afford for Mom to go to the home. The sanatorium. It was called The Parks. Which makes you think of green rolling lawns and tranquil spaces, but the first time I went there, this guy screamed and screamed like a scared child. There was nothing calm and quiet about it.

Orderlies in white jackets had to restrain him to sedate him. It was all pretty traumatizing.

The Parks was an old, converted house in the country with big steel-fashioned gates that automatically closed behind you. Jo came with me once. She said it reminded her of that haunted house series where a family who flips houses buy the wrong house, and their kids are traumatized, one by one, by the ghosts that live there.

I remember her telling me that because it was literally the worst comparison she could've made.

She didn't know that though.

I always tell people that Mom had issues with her nerves. Highly strung. Anxious. On edge.

I've said it so many times there's a part of me that thinks that's the truth. But of course, it isn't.

I didn't tell Jo. I don't tell anyone.

Some things are better in than out.

Today, I'm on time for school. Joe's at the top of the

stairs. This time, he's talking to the redhead. Should I loiter and give them their space?

He spots me and half-raises his hand in greeting.

It's a start.

"Let's hear some appreciation for this major accomplishment," I announce as I reach the two of them. "On time, within the first bell. And properly attired."

Jeans, basic T-shirt, basic jacket. Basic, basic, basic. A blending-in day rather than a standing-out one.

"I liked your top yesterday," says the redhead. "The one with the cute green monster."

"The Kid," corrects Joe. "That's his name."

The redhead is all kinds of shades of pink.

"I haven't seen the show yet," I lie. It's iconic and I've devoured it more than once. "Thank you for the bags yesterday. I owe you."

"You're welcome. Anytime." She chews on the skin of her thumbnail. "Greg had to miss our lab session to finish his band practice, so we didn't use ours yet."

"Grace here is the smartest student at Pinedale," says Joe. There's a definite pride in his voice. "We go way back."

"That's kind of you to say." Her gaze has dropped to the floor, and she's making patterns with her shoes on the concrete. "I just like to read. That's all. Most people prefer to game, like Joe." There's a sweet, teasing note in her voice. When she looks up at him, she's all wide eyes and expectation.

Whoa, she's got it but bad. Joe is Captain Oblivious.

I bridge the awkward gap that's developing. "What do you like to read?"

"Romantasy."

My blank stare prompts her. "It's fairies and elves

and magical worlds. Sometimes, we even dress up."

Joe raises his eyebrows.

Grace winds it back in again. "Only for cons and stuff, not like for every day. That would be weird." She pulls on the straps of her backpack. "I better get going. Joe, text me when you want your…supply."

My turn to raise my eyebrows.

"It's not what you think." Joe immediately catches my rampant imagination about to leap into full flight. "I'm not going into it. But it's not what you think."

"Whatevs. You have your life, I have mine."

Far be it for me to pry.

Though I'm curious.

Most schools have their resident dealers. You have to know the right person to ask. Somehow, I never would have thought of someone like Grace. She seems so…well brought up? Oh, that's patronizing. Sensible? That's also patronizing. Not her thing? Well, dealing is not doing.

Nervous? That's more like it. Nervy.

"You ready to tackle English?" asks Joe. "You're in time for *Northanger Abbey.*"

I turn up my nose. "What's that? Some horrible verb declension?"

He almost smiles. "Jane Austen."

"Never heard of her."

We amble to class. I mentally note the twists and turns so I don't get lost.

"Made it and with time to spare," I say as we find the English class that I couldn't locate for love or money or followers on my last attempt. "I'm going to use the bathroom."

Joe's already talking to some jock mate of his.

We're on time, and he wouldn't care if I said I was going to jump off the building, stark naked.

One glance at the bathroom door, and my heart does a skip. It's the senior girls' bathroom. I've found it!

The same thick smell of bleach and cherry greets me, only this time, someone's been smoking actual cigs in here too, lending the place a more-ashy afterburn.

Sam's leaning over the sink, their hair under the tap—faucet.

"You're here!" I do a happy dance. "I've been looking for you all over."

"Right here, babe."

"Ah, I had this…" I refrain from completing my sentence. It was a dream, see? Nothing to be worrying about. There's no harm done. Sam is all good. In one piece. No sign of any traumatic brain injury. "Nah, I…what you doing?"

"Trying to dye my bangs blue." They separate strands of wet hair with their fingers. Bangs. Not fringe. Their black lips are the same black as the other day, glossier though. I wonder if they took my suggestion about the eyeliner?

Sam groans. "Does it look like it's working?"

"Honestly? No." Platinum more than blue. In fact, there's no blue at all. "Maybe you should try more of the blue toner? Leave it on for longer?"

"It's been a half hour already."

Sam's dressed in what can only be described as a plumber's overall. A full-on one-piece. Gold sneakers and…

My blood runs cold.

Pom-poms. Shocking-pink pom-pom socks.

Chapter 15

Big dreams

"I can't wait to leave Pinedale." Sam rinses out the dye from their hair. "It's so…parochial."

"What does that mean?" I'm still reeling from the sight of those pom-poms. That's quite the detail my subconscious dug up. Unless they were wearing them when I first met them, and I didn't see them, but my subconscious did. See? Logical explanation.

"Parochial? Like narrow. Tiny. Small town. Everyone knows everyone, everyone knows everyone's business." They sigh. "It's all I've ever dreamed of. To finish high school and blow this popsicle stand sky high. Hit the road, head to New York. Then Vogue."

"Oh wow." They sound so sure, so certain.

"Yeah, Anna Wintour, eat your heart out."

"It's not like she just got there." My joke lies flat where I dropped it. I switch my tone. Maybe my sarcasm isn't translating. "She's fashion royalty, though. The Queen. The Met Ball and all that? I'd kill for a ticket to see those outfits up close and personal."

Sam gives me an odd look and then shakes their head. "I guess it's an English thing. Met ball? Yeah, luv? Such a kidder."

Somewhere, I've lost this conversation. Never fear, I will track back. "Do you want to be a stylist? Or…?"

They squeeze the water out of their tired hair. Yep, still platinum. "Whatever I can get, honey. All the names, all the fashion I could eat for breakfast, that's what I want. To be in it. Part of it. And New York, baby. Anything goes. The city that never sleeps. The nightlife, oh my God. It's calmed down some with the epidemic, still, it's not like here. Nothing like here. Freedom. You can be who you want. No apologies."

"What's the difference between an epidemic and a pandemic? You're the first I've heard call it an epidemic."

"Beats me. Either way, you don't want it."

I can't argue with that.

"It didn't take." Another sigh. Sam eyes my hair. "Is that permed?"

"No, this is it, *au naturel*. I sometimes put in gel. Live dangerously."

They're checking me out from all sides. "You could do with some height in front. Look at those curls, though. Without a perm? Honey, you are lucky. I sat in the salon for hours with that developer on my head, and the smell? Lord have mercy. Where's your pirate pants today?"

"Retired. Straight-up denim instead."

"Is that stretch in those pants?"

"Yeah, it's always a stretch blend."

"Since when?" They stop smoothing down their damp fringe, sorry, *bangs*. "If I had stretch in my pants, I wouldn't need to work the sewing machine. I still have to lie on the bed to get my zipper up."

"Say what? I squeeeeeeeze in, then let it relax. God bless stretch."

There's that confused look again. "Londontown is clearly ahead of the times."

"You were wearing leggings the other day?" They were, weren't they? "With stirrups." I remember that much.

"Ski pants?"

"I guess." Back to the red block, yellow block, blue block conundrum. It's as if they're speaking an entirely different language. Different from American English too. Like we're in two different places altogether. "So I'm part of the photography club now."

"Look at you. Over those first-days blues already." Sam's smile is broad and genuine.

I feel ten feet tall. They're like the older sister I never had. We could swap clothes, do each other's make-up, do the dances together on the toc.

Sam finishes styling their fringe, sorry, *bangs*, and fixes their attention to their eyebrows. "My mom got me one of those instant cameras that spit out immediately. I blew through my allowance on film. I took photos of my different looks, put them in an album. For my records. So I've got something to show when I make my grand entrance at Vogue's headquarters."

For some reason, my mind turns to my mom. She had photo albums crammed with printed photos she'd taken of herself and her friends at school. Some of the pages had movie ticket stubs or invitations to parties. Kind of like scrapbooking. But not. They used to gather dust in the loft at home. They're now making their way into the basement. To also gather dust.

"But then my mom said I better save up money for bus fare, or I'm going nowhere." They pluck stray hairs from under their already perfect eyebrows. "I'll arrive by bus, but I'm coming back in a sleek black limousine."

"You're so lucky, you know what you want to do.

Everyone keeps asking me, and I have no idea." My insides twist up and solidify. "It feels like a big wide nothing out there."

"Don't you worry, Little Miss Lila, you'll find your thing. You already have style, that's without question. What's your bag?"

"My bag?"

"Yeah, my mom always says that. What's your thing? Your special talent?"

"I don't think I have one."

"Everyone has one. You'll figure it out."

It's hard to describe how much I don't want to figure it out. If I look forward, there's honestly nothing but a vast grey landscape. There's no path, no road, no nothing. Just the greyness. I don't like to look out there. At the nothing.

Sam puts their arm around me. "Honey, don't you worry now. The future will be there. No need to rush to find it."

The pain behind my eyeballs digs in. This happens sometimes. I'll be feeling a-okay, and then this wave of sadness barrels through me. If I try to stop it, it thickens and clogs up. It hurts like something heavy's pushing on my chest with hot pokers.

But I swallow the sadness back. "We ran into the Bruno Brothers again. Me and Joe."

Sam gives me a last squeeze and lets me go. "My condolences. That's some bad news. You get out of it, okay?"

"They threw Joe's books around. It was so...childish. Like the kind of pranks your kid brother would play."

"I don't have one of those. Only-child blues.

"Me too."

We share a smile.

Sam returns to their eyebrows. "Rumor has it they started a fire here. Those brothers. Burned half the school down. You can still see the remnants on the far side of the school. They have made some repairs, though. Over on the red block."

That shocks me to my core. "And they're still here? At the school?"

"Like I said, a rumor."

"Was everyone okay?"

"No, some students died, I think."

"What? What in the actual hell? And they're still allowed to be here?" My mind can't wrap around it. "You set fire to a school, kill people, like dead, and you're allowed to be on the grounds, picking on other students?"

Sam gives me that confused look for a third time. Am I saying something wrong? Is it okay to kill students here on a Friday and return for lessons the following Monday? What does the counsellor, Mrs. False Eyelashes, say? Or the principal? Why do they have this weird inclusion policy if they allow arsonists on the property?

"It wasn't proven it was them." Sam shrugs. "It's merely suspected. It's too late now, either way."

"But, that's...crazy."

Yo, *that* word again.

It dawns on me slowly then in a rush. "Oh my God, I've been chatting in here like I'm not supposed to be in class right now. I'm going to be late for English again. Joe is going to kill me."

"I'll catch you up later," assures Sam.

Good. There's clearly a big hole in this school's logic that I'm missing.

Chapter 16

The picture's developing

My phone beeps. It's Tomas, the intrepid photographer. His profile pic is of a multi-eyed alien cat. Which reminds me that I must do the door-to-door thing and find Fuzzwhat's home. Before my father notices that I haven't. It's hard to hide a kitten, even one that disappears in the shadows. They mew.

—*Your turn to develop this avvie. Don't spill.*—

Oh. Okay then.

I could have sworn he said that we'd do the developing thing together at the next meeting. My stomach flips over. If those guys can develop, I can develop. I tell myself this over and over, and it does nothing to address the can of upended worms in my gut.

I've looked it up.

The developing, not the worms in my gut.

Three chemicals seem to be key. Three chemical baths, to be more specific. And you have to be in the dark. The mythical darkroom.

So long as helpful people post their handy how-to videos, I can hustle my way through. How else do I know how to contour my cheeks for that super snatched look? Or to level up my outfit to a banging look?

I don't have anyone to ask, but those videos are right there. A true gift from the universe.

Joe is texting with a fury next to me.

His thumbs jitter.

I'm in the dog box again after managing to get myself locked out of English.

"You will be at the lab at three tomorrow," he's now said to me, texted me, instant messaged me, and I bet, if I checked, emailed me.

Yes, yes, yes. *Yes.*

I'll be there.

On time.

Such a nagger. He must run on pure adrenaline.

The final bell rings.

He's out the door faster than a dog hearing the treat bag open.

Grace waves at me.

I wave back, hopeful that it was, in fact, at me and not at someone else standing behind me.

But then she comes over. "How's the school treating you?"

"Relatively well. The pupils and the staff, however…"

She cracks a smile. "That bad?"

"You wouldn't believe it."

"You want to hang out sometime?"

Part of me wonders if she wants to pump for information about my buddy, Joe. I dismiss the thought. "Sure, that would be great."

She adds my phone number and sends me a missed call. "I've got cheer practice. Later."

A beat of excitement stirs. A friend. Maybe. *The smartest girl in school.* That's not daunting at all. My marks are good, but no one has confused me for the smartest girl in school.

I scuttle down to the photography club.

Little tin shack on the prairie.

Tomas has left me a series of notes tacked to the back of the door.

Use the safelight.

The trays are marked.

Your film is on the shelf.

Don't waste the paper.

Two prints maximum.

Don't spill the chemicals.

Use the tongs.

The pegs are in the drawer.

Have fun. Don't stay out late. Don't do anything I would do. Yes, Dad.

Where to start?

There is indeed one plastic film cylinder sitting lonely as can be on the metal shelving. Three trays. A set of tongs. And photographic paper.

I could bail, right here and now.

But.

Curiosity is beckoning. Inside that plastic cylinder are 24 possible photos, black and white, as it turns out, and until I dip the film into those three trays, they'll remain a mystery.

I switch on the safelight, and I'm bathed in a red glow.

I roll up my sleeves, prop up my phone, and take a huge breath.

First things first, the enlarger to choose which photos I'll print.

Feeding through the film is easier than expected. The photos, though, need work. There's a blur. Oh, and another one. I must have clicked and moved at the same time. There's a fun one of a pack of students laughing near the lockers. It makes my maybe list.

A photo of my foot. Hmmm.

One of the inside of my bag.

So much for not wasting film. Brian will have a fit.

A shot of the principal chewing out a student. It's clear, in focus, in the frame, and not at all student-centric.

I skip over the next and the next.

Stop. Wait. That one.

It's the building Sam said was in the fire. The red block, as they called it. I've managed to capture a single student gazing up at the rebuilt remains. There's a sense of nostalgia I can't really put my finger on. Like it's about a different time and place. But school's the same.

I can't unjumble my thoughts into coherence.

There's a *feeling* behind the shot. A kind of longing that's reaching out to me.

Isn't that what Zook or Brian or Tomas had been whittering about?

With unsteady hands, I adjust the lens to enlarge the photo. It takes a fair amount of zooming in and out, like trying to negotiate the Maps app on your phone. The paper's a solid letter size, and the negative is teeny-weeny tiny.

The building's outline dissolves, and the student takes center stage.

I enlarge again. And again.

It can't be...

I would have noticed.

I took the photo, after all.

A series of cold chills goosebump down my spine.

Impossible.

I was there.

The student's face swings into focus. It's the blond member of the Bruno Brothers gang. There's no question. The slicked-back hair, the jacket, the boots.

And he's looking right at me.

I pull away from the viewfinder.

Don't be ridiculous. It's a photo. It's not going to hurt me.

He's not in the enlarger!

I glance behind me. The door's still closed. There's no one there.

My tutorial video is happily blathering on explaining how to make your print. It's a solid reminder of what's real. Logical. Explainable.

If I didn't notice him when I took the photo, it was because I was nervous of harming Tomas's camera. I was concentrating on the light and shadow of the building. I was thinking about how lousy my first day at this school had been.

That's why.

It was one of those perfectly logical explanations.

My heart's jackhammering, though.

It doesn't buy the logic. *You would have seen him.*

But I didn't.

An overwhelming urge to run out of this darkroom, the school, and never turn back grips me.

Calm down. Take a breath. Take a whole big mouthful of a rest.

Something's not right here.

Two prints. I make my choices.

My attention is back to the task at hand, and I transfer my first print from the developer, stop, and then fix trays. Not too bad.

It's the one of the students. A candid shot. Happy,

relaxed, at ease. A snapshot of everyday school life. High school yearbook style.

My three colleagues will hate its guts. With a visceral passion. And much self-deprecation.

Now for the second.

I let it sit in the developer until every line is crisp and clear, the dark/light balance as close to perfect as my amateur eye can get it. Then I scoop it up into the stop tray.

It's the blond, all right.

Yes, he's looking at me.

And he's pointing back at the building.

Chapter 17

Black kitty magic

Fuzzwhat screeches the place down the second I open the front door. Their eye's still a little weepy. They need a vet.

Before I can procrastinate any further, I gather them up and head next door.

The clutter of kids' toys on the porch impedes my progress to the doorbell. Fuzzwhat perches on my shoulder, their baby claws digging in for traction. It hurts like a mother.

I rehearse what I'm going to say. *Hi, I'm from next door. I found this kitten under the apple tree. Is it yours?*

There's a tug to my heart that I'm pretending is not there.

"We're not taking any strays", says a voice from inside. Did they watch me walk up here? I didn't even press the doorbell.

"Oh, I wasn't looking to give any away."

"No strays."

I switch Fuzzwhat to my other shoulder and almost go straight home. I try the next house. No one home but a huge aggro dog chained up and charging at me from their yard.

Those claws are drawing blood, and they're hissing and spitting in my ear at the sight of the dog. "Don't worry, little fluff, pretty sure this isn't your home."

Two houses more. That's fair for today, right? Enough of an effort. Proof that I did go and look. When Dad asks, I can say I tried.

The next house has some ancient guy mowing the lawn. He sees me coming and shakes his head at me.

One more house and it's done.

"Hey, Lila B, what you doin' out here?"

It's Grace. She's sitting on the porch of the house one over.

Attempts to remove Fuzzwhat from my shoulder are unsuccessful. How is something that small so strong? I couldn't get them to loosen their grip with pliers. Not that I'd try, either. "Don't suppose you're missing your kitten?"

"Nu-uh. We've got two. Jasmine and George. They're in their beds upstairs." Grace wanders over to me. She's in her cheerleading outfit, and the skirt bounces as much as her hair. "Hey, little guy." She easily lifts Fuzzwhat from me and flips them over for a belly rub. "Oh, it's a little girl."

"Ah, that solves that mystery. They say to look under their tail, but I don't know what I'm looking for."

"Balls."

"I asked for that. I found her in a tree," I point in the direction of my house. "Trying to see who she belongs to."

"Judging from the eye and the ribs, I'd say she's been dumped. Were there others?"

"Just her."

"Congratulations, you've got yourself a kitty." Fuzzwhat is putty in her hands. "There's a vet practice two blocks up, and she can help with the eye."

"Thank you. I don't think my dad will let me keep her, though."

"He doesn't like cats?"

"It's complicated."

"People say that when it's not really, they don't want to admit the truth to themselves."

I digest this. "You're probably right."

Fuzzwhat has wrapped her tiny body around Grace's hand. "It's so much easier to say it's complicated though, because you can convince yourself it is, and it stops the other person from asking any more questions."

"Joe's right, you are the smartest girl in the school."

There's a sadness in her expression. "Not smart. It's..."

"Complicated?"

She gives me a shy smile. "You can always put a notice up on the community boards if you want to. Anyone over forty looks at those. I don't think anyone's coming to look for her, though. Her right ear's flopping, and she's missing some fur on her belly. Look, see."

"Now I feel like a bad parent."

"My mother used to trap ferals. I've learned a thing or two, that's all. She's young too. I'd say about five weeks. Does she chew your hair?"

"At night? Yes."

"She's been abandoned." The statement makes me want to hide this kitten in my ribcage where it's warm and safe and no one can ever hurt her again.

Fuzzwhat remembers who she is and starts up with the squawking.

Grace hands her back to me. The mewing stops when I put her back on my shoulder.

"Looks like she knows who mom is. Maybe she's

your familiar?"

"My what?"

"A familiar. A guardian or a protector. There's any number of explanations. Some say it's a spirit that's in the form of an animal. Others say it's a divine intervention to help someone communicate with the next world. I say it's an animal that's on your wavelength, the one that gets you, that you have a special bond with. That's my George to me. He's my shadow."

There's a slippery feeling over her words. My mind goes back to that photo. Of the dream I had about Sam. And now all this talk about cats that can see into the afterlife. It seems…medieval. Cats like food, warmth, more food, big attention—on their terms— and more food. They're not busy chatting with dead people and passing on messages to the living. Even if they can see the dead, like my mom said.

Fuzzwhat's eyeballing the man with the mower. "Pretty sure I'll have to give this one up by the end of the week."

Grace shrugs. "I call it kitty magic. No matter how bad my day is, George is there. He meets me on the walk home from school, he curls up next to me, he's always there. You're never lonely with a familiar."

Why does every word feel like a bullet to the chest? "Yeah, well, maybe I can work on my dad."

"How did your biology trip go? Joe's the top biology student. Has been for years. He's passionate about protecting our woods and wildlife."

Oh, I was right. Grace has a huge, thumping crush on Joe. Fact.

Her cheeks flush whenever she says his name.

"We got a lot of samples. Correction. He got a lot of

samples. I watched for bears."

"We took from right by the fence. I didn't have time with cheering and my grandfather. He lives with us. It's his house, actually. I take the afternoon shift after school. He can't really walk."

"I get it. Sometimes I had to watch my mom…"

Grace nods. "I don't mind doing it, but it makes things very…real. It's difficult to talk about fun things when your mom's shouting about adult diapers. Or money."

"I hear you."

"So the vet will give you a discount if you ask. She's really kind. I better get going. He likes to have his first beer about now. Good luck with the kitty."

"Fuzzwhat."

"Oh, you've already named her." She gives me a sly smile, which I pretend to ignore. "You're in deep, and you don't even know it."

For the smartest girl, Grace knows nothing.

Chapter 18

Hold my hand

I'm at dearly beloved Pinedale High.

There's a fear in me that has me on my tippy-toes. Imagine? Me. On my tippys, like some ballerina. Like some chick.

It's so cold a bear needs a fur coat. All I got is my jacket and those few shots we had before we got here from Jack's place out on the tracks. They don't ask for ID there.

There's a strange smell in the air. I don't like it. I don't like anything about this setup.

I'm looking for someone. They're not supposed to be here. I'm not supposed to be here either. Dark figures circle. Teachers. Chaperones? Police, even.

The authorities. Always there. Always ruining a good time.

There's a bottle of cheap sweet sherry in my back pocket. It's full and feels like I'm carrying the ending of my school career. The fear is revving louder in my ears. Can't they hear me skulking out here? I can hear a cricket farting.

For sure, they can hear me out here. Any second now, they'll take me in, and it will be overs kadovers.

I could hide the bottle in the bushes. Say I'm keeping it for a friend. Well, that's partially true. It's not mine.

I told 'em it was a bad idea, but Charlie doesn't like to listen. What does he think those flaps of skin are for? Decoration? Wind up your ears, Charlie, and let me tell you good, this was a stinking bad idea.

I wanna go to college. He doesn't get that.

School. It's just a formality. It's not the end of your life.

He says a whole lotta baloney about taking the train out to his brother's on the coast and workin' on some movies, but I gotta tell ya, that's not what I want.

Stability. A decent paycheck. I don't wanna bust my butt working at some factory all my days, like my old man. I wanna job in the city. You need to be a college man for that. And they don't much like kids who had their asses expelled for—

Geez Louise, my legs are filled with lead. How come I can't run here? It's like I'm in cement boots.

Of course, Charlie's big plan was a bust.

Those jocks deserve a boot in the ass, I don't disagree. But setting firecrackers off across the football field? Just plain stupid. He had some other cousin rig them up, so with one flick of his lighter, boom, boom, boom. Firework city.

Sure, it was funny watching them crash into each other—more than usual. We had our fun.

But no, not Charlie. He wanted something...bigger. Something that would really stick it to 'em.

The building's getting no closer. I'm running, man, really working on my lungs here.

Oh, it's one of those dreams.

Another dream.

It's the building from my photo. It's different.

Bigger. Almost twice, three times the size. Double-volume. There's a light on inside. Scattered lights, colored lights. A party? A dance?

Something's wrong.

Something's very wrong.

Charlie said if anything happened, to split. Get the hell out of there. His words.

Why the hell can't I run any faster?

The main entrance is blocked.

There's a side entrance to the building, and I tear open the door.

I suck on black smoke.

My eyes sting.

My lungs tar black.

Fire. There's a fire.

In the building.

We didn't. *I didn't*. It can't be those firecrackers. Those were kid stuff. A snap, a crackle. Nothing doing.

Yeah, but Charlie—

No, I don't want to be in someone else's dream. What's going on? My heart's racing faster than my chest.

Have to get him out. He's gotta be here. Why's it taking so long to find the gym? Biggest space in the whole goddamn school, and I can't even stumble on it. Every cough is a choke.

A hand grabs my shoulder, and I'm ready to smack them on the nose.

"What you doin', man?" It's Eugene. His words clam up in the smoke. "You wanna get yourself killed?"

"Beau's in there, I gotta try get him out."

"You need to get offa the school property before they haul your ass to jail."

It's like someone opened the oven door. A wall of heat shimmies around us. I'd gag for some of that cool air about now. "They can haul out my dead body first."

"You don't wanna do this, Evan." Charlie's more of a mirage than a real person. "Do like I said, drop the fuse, then head over to Jack's till the heat dies down."

"Are you crazy? You've set the school on fire."

Charlie raises his arms all innocent-like. "Nuthin to do with me, man."

"My brother's in there." Yeah, and these two brothers are acting like it's no big deal. Screw them.

I try to cover my mouth and nose with my arm, my jacket, anything. I can feel the flames. The heat's starting to get to me, but man, the smoke. That's something else. It's burning in tracks down my lungs.

Charlie's voice is behind me.

I've gotta find Beau. My dad will kill me if anything happens to him. I'll kill me if anything happens to him. He's not supposed to be here. My knees went all kinds of weak when I saw him there in the stands. He's got no interest in sports. What's he doin' there?

And then the fireworks went off, pah, pah, pah.

It all happened so fast.

Eugene dragged my ass out.

And then, and then…I can't really catch my breath.

Can't see where I'm going. "I'm coming, Beau, I'm coming." He's only twelve. A junior, for chrissakes. A little kid. Whole life right there.

And I go and mess it up.

Eugene's shouting something, I don't know what.

Screw these guys. I'm done with 'em.

When I get out of here, I'm finished. No more. It's not fun. It's mean.

If I can find Beau…

There are flames, flames everywhere.

I wake up with a start. I open my mouth and take a gulp of air. The back of my neck's wet with sweat. So's the space under my knees and in the small of my back. Drenched wet.

I steady my breathing.

What. The hell. Was that?

Charlie. Eugene. The Bruno Brothers.

Evan. The blond. I was him. Or he was me.

His dream. That was *his* dream. Just like it was Sam's.

I mentally sift through the dream's images.

They'd felt so…real.

It's your mind. It can't tell the difference between what's real and what's not.

I pick up my phone and start to doomscroll on the toc.

Thoughts deep into how to curl your hair with a bendy thing that sits like an Alice band, then a dupe test for an airbrush foundation, before sliding into a quick meal you can make in a single pot with five not-so-handy ingredients.

It's the anxiety of the move, the changes, everything's different and that's okay.

I wish my mom was here.

No. You know what she'd say.

I scroll to the next video.

It's almost daybreak by the time I put my phone back down on the nightstand.

Chapter 19

Lab partners

First, Sam and now...*Evan*. That's what his name
was in the dream. The blond greaser. Logically, the
dream originated from talk about the Bruno brothers
setting fire to the school. Combine that with the photo,
and bam! My brain raced through its most anxiety-
provoking possibilities and spat out that one.

Thank you once again, my little subconscious, for
freaking me out.

Two dreams, though.

Clearly, my stress levels are working overtime.

Have I sorted out the kitten? No.

I bet there'll be a dream tonight or tomorrow about
how I have to give up the kitten or else some creature
from the woods will hunt me down and—

Let me pause on that thought.

My imagination is far too vivid.

I don't want to encourage nightmares in.

"Where have you been?" Joe looks up from the lab
desk, our soil samples lined up in front of him, ready for
action. Judging from the state of things, he's been here a
whole while.

"Yes, I'm late. I couldn't remember which block it
was and ended up in the library." I clamber onto the stool
next to him. "Maybe they *should* have red blocks, yellow

blocks, blue blocks."

"That only works if you're not color blind."

"I didn't think of that." There's still the unanswered question of why Sam mentioned them in the first place. If they didn't exist. "What can I help with?"

"Grab some of those beakers and heat them up to sterilize them."

"Over the burner? Do I have to light it?"

"It won't burn unless you turn on the gas."

I pull up my big-girl panties. Talk of burning and fire feels close to the bone. "How many beakers."

"Enough for the samples."

"There are more samples than beakers."

"Can never have enough samples." He's intent on pipetting solution in measured droplets into his beaker. He says each word very slowly in time with the dropping. I bet he makes his bed every morning before school.

Not one to bother a genius at work, I confront the Bunsen burner. Turn on the gas. That ominous hissing fills me with dread. I light the match. Turn off the gas. I wasn't ready. C'mon. I can do hard things. It's not like I'll burn down the school. Bad analogy.

One, two, three, gas on. Light a match and...poof. A blue flame. Success.

I swill the flame around the inside of a few beakers. If Joe's looking for perfection, he must do it himself.

Soon enough, I too am pipetting solution into the soil samples in my freshly sterilized beakers.

"The soil here's really good. Lots of nutrients." I note down the results. "Any of these three here would be good for the aquarium."

"Yeah, it's gonna be a hard choice to make. But

good to have that many choices."

"I concur. Lack of choice has been the story of my life."

"Tell me about it."

I nearly drop my pipette. "You had to leave your home and fly across the world to a completely different country and leave behind everyone you knew and loved, and had no say whatsoever. I mean, I might be projecting here?"

Is that some suppressed anger rising to the surface? Never.

"That's rough. When you put it that way." He wipes away chemical solution with a neatly squared paper towel. He doesn't swish it away, oh no. He pushes forward, then to the right, then to the left, then back again. "My parents have expectations…that's all."

"Thought you were all set to be an environmental scientist."

"That's what I want to do, yes. It's why I need a scholarship. Then I get a choice." *Blip, blip*. He drips the solution. "They say that college is a golden noose. I'd be better off working in the family business."

"What's that?"

"Car sales."

"Used?"

"No, it's a big dealership. I'm just not into cars. Not like they are." He makes a note on his phone. "I'm like my dad with the football and all. But there's this other part that's more interested in plants and ecology, the ocean, you know? I don't want to sell cars. They're part of the problem." He flushes. "I don't know why I'm telling you this."

"You're not alone. Ever since I was a kid, I'd have

people give me their true confessions. Standing in a queue, waiting for my coffee order, using the wishy-washy."

"The what?"

"Laundry. Laundrette? Jo's mom used to send us down there to start the load off. Jo's my best friend."

"Same name as me."

I hadn't noticed until this exact second. "Maybe your dad will change his mind."

"He's not that kind of guy. He's very…rigid."

Hmmm. Joe has more in common with his father than he knows. I guess we all have our blind spots.

His face screws up. "You smell that? Did you turn off the gas?"

I fly off the stool. "Shit!"

"Yeah, wouldn't be good if you burned down the school."

The gas is indeed humming away. I switch it off. "Especially since it had a recent incident."

"What do you mean?"

"There was a fire recently? Some students? Playing with firecrackers? The football team? A dance?"

There's that familiar look of confusion. Just when I thought I was making progress. Like my English was the same as everyone else's.

He corrects me. "You mean the fire of '53?"

"No, recently."

"The only one I know of is the fire of '53. Most of the school burned down, and it took a whole lot of students with it. It's that building near the fields. I don't know about students starting it, though. I heard it was a fire in the woods that ran through."

A familiar chill rushes up my spine. "1953? Like a

hundred years ago?"

"Not quite a hundred. But, yeah."

Why did Sam say the Bruno brothers tried to burn down the school? That dream sits uncomfortably in any conclusions I'm drawing. They were there. All three of them.

1953?

Yep, those chills were multiplying and growing feelers.

I feel…blindsided. I don't know what to say. "My father never mentioned there was a fire here."

"The school's been standing a while. I only know about it because we had to do an extra-credit project on the school's history."

And he's never heard of the Bruno brothers either.

"You look like you've seen a ghost."

I shake my head. "There's no such thing."

Then he says something that makes no sense.

"With Pinedale, you never know."

Chapter 20

Oopsie-daisy

The weekend whooshed past me. I blinked, and I missed it.

What's with those two days hyperventilating past at the speed of light?

I might have hid Fuzzwhat in my room.

I might have stared at that photo with Evan for a lot longer than was probably sane.

I definitely ruminated on Joe's words.

My dad spent most of his time watching old movies and drinking new beer.

I spent most of my time in my room, not unpacking and wishing I was somewhere else.

Monday morning, it was back-to-school time.

I've figured out the kind of uniform they wear here. Oversized jacket, crop top, jeans. Boots mostly. Eyebrows. Glossy lip.

Got it.

There's no Joe waiting for me.

It's okay.

He's definitely defrosting. Friendlier. More open. Less scowly.

I also realise I'm the only one who feels that way about Joe. They see Captain Sunshine. I see Mr. Grump-a-lump.

First class is History. I locate the class, no problem. There are no run-ins with the Bruno Brothers. No books upended, no feet tripped, no ties pulled or necks snapped. That might be an exaggeration, but the dream suggested they did set off crackers round those footballers' feet. Doesn't that sound psycho to you?

A dream. Yes. Yes, you're right.

Only a dream.

The photo of Evan and the building is in my bag. I have to hang it up in the club room. So that it can be critiqued at our next meeting.

Yay. Looking so forward to that.

I wave at Grace, who sits in the front of the class.

She bounds over. "Did you get Fuzzwhat to the vet?"

"Not in as many words."

"So you didn't? How's her eye?"

"Better." It's not better. It's worse. I have to tell my dad about her, I do. But he's going to tell me to take her to the SPCA and drop her off. They'll put her down if she doesn't get a home. And right now, she has a home. My bedroom. Although the litter tray is getting kind of nasty.

I'll tell him. I will.

"How was your weekend?"

Grace frowns. "Gramps had a bit of a turn. But he's okay now." She's visibly paler, like a vampire swung in for a schlurp or two. "We thought he'd be taken."

"Taken?"

"Passed away."

"Oh, dead."

"Yeah. Passed away."

"Dead." Sorry, but my mother did not pass away.

She didn't fade until she disappeared. The opposite. She roared, and sobbed, and begged, and fought, and scratched the walls until her fingernails bled. But she didn't pass.

Her body gave up.

And, poof, she was released. The thing, a soul, whatever you want to call it, it left and the meat remained. Jo said I always sound dramatic when I say it like that. I don't know how else to say it. One moment, she was there. The next, she'd gone.

There was no sense of time f-a-d-i-n-g between the two.

Here. Gone.

"Are you okay, Lila? You seem a bit spacey." Grace's voice tracks me back to the here and now. Part of me was in my mother's room at the sanatorium. Maybe part of me always would be there. At that moment.

"Groovy two-shoes," I answer.

"What's that?"

"I don't know. Someone said it in the lunch queue the other day, right before someone else told them not to 'have a cow.' "

"What does that even mean?"

"You tell me! I've never heard so many strange expressions. I mean, 'don't have a cow'? What is that even? Who would have a cow?"

"Definitely sus."

"Some other guy asked me, 'Can I dig it?' Like, what?"

"Are you serious?"

"Dead. And he had on this weird-ass fur hat."

Grace looks as baffled as I feel. "A fur hat?"

"Big round thing. Looked real too." I exaggerate the shape and size with my hands. "Like he was harboring a few dead rats on his head."

She laughed. "Maybe he was."

There's a comfortable lull. We both watch Joe stride into the room, give us a nod, yes, both of us, and head for his seat. Grace keeps looking for longer than deemed socially acceptable in my book.

I pick up the conversation. "But seriously, is your grandfather going to be okay?"

She shrugs. "What's okay? He can't walk too well, he can't see for shit, his hearing is shot. Hopefully, he'll stick around a bit longer. He says he wants to see me graduate first. He went here too. Back in the day."

"No kidding? So did my dad."

Grace sighs as if she's a hundred years old. "Does anyone ever leave Pinedale?"

That's a depressing thought.

Sam wants to get out of here. Joe's got big plans. I'm still playing "When I lived in London…"

Maybe some of us never get out of here.

The teacher's arrival signals the end of our catch-up.

Before I head to my seat near Joe, I risk straight-up loserdom. "Do you want to sit with me at lunch?"

"Thanks, Lila, but I've got a cheer meeting. Maybe tomorrow?"

Baby steps.

Making friends here is not like back home. I'm the newbie. An unknown entity.

I still haven't seen Sam in the cafeteria. Besides, they're a senior.

Baby steps.

I'm getting used to my eat-for-one meals at

107

lunchtime.

Sometimes, I blitz in and out of there, as if I have somewhere more important to be. Then I amble to the library and pore over their old fashion and beauty books from the '90s.

Other times, I eat super slowly, like I'm really enjoying every moment of the experience, lost in my own thoughts. But actually, I'm listening to my music, my collar concealing my earbud.

Like I said, baby steps.

The morning scoots by. Grace says she'll catch up later, which is reassuring. Joe reminds me that we have to go scoop some more soil. He's not happy with some of our results. Sigh. Such a perfectionist.

I head for the cafeteria. I have the drill now. I am unstoppable.

I take my time, choose my drink, an orange juice, then slide into the queue. I make my choices, chili—I have no idea what this is—and there's chocolate pudding.

Am I on the lookout for Evan? You bet. Fortunately, there's been no sidling up to me since that first day.

Armed with my lunch, I make the move to find a spare seat. Let's correct that. A spare table.

If I get here early enough, I can tuck on the end of an empty table and not bother anyone at all. A quick scour of the scene reveals no Sam. No Joe. And no empty table.

There are three empty seats. A group of girls. Younger.

I can do this. *Hi, mind if I sit here? Hey, there. May I?*

It happens so fast I can't wrap my head around the

details.

One moment, I'm heading purposefully toward the table. The next? My foot pulls back and...*stays there*. Trapped. Stuck. My body launches forward. But there's the tray. I can't drop the tray. I can't use my hands either. It doesn't matter, though, because I'm f-a-l-l-i-n-g. Whatever's jamming my foot moves away. And I slap face-first down into the tiles. My knees wince. The tray remains aloft a second longer, then slams, bam.

Splosh! Chilli and chocolate pudding splurge up before splashing down. It spatters all over me like that artist who threw paint from his brush onto a canvas. Only no one will be throwing millions at me for this particular artwork.

There's an interminable pause.

And then I hear it. The unmistakable sound of the Brunos' laughter echoes behind me.

Just when I thought it was safe to go back into the cafeteria...

The laughter increases. My inner rage rocks up and unleashes, tasting of chili and watery chocolate pudding. "Why don't you leave me alone? What the hell is wrong with all of you?"

I wipe dripping chilli off my face, my neck and, ohmygod, it's in my hair, webbing in between the strands. I will not cry. I will not cry.

"We warned you. Stick with your own kind, but no, you had to go and mix with *them*." It's Charlie who says that. He's uglier in the flesh than my dream remembers. Next to him, Eugene clutches his sides.

"Ah, yes, this is sooo hil-a-ri-ous." I mock. "Maybe this is what you think is amusing out here, but where I come from, this is bollocks bullshit. You hideous, miserable bullies."

My hands are ill-equipped to scoop up the mess. The sole serviette I took is already sodden.

Charlie stands in the upended chili. He looks down, down, down at me and sneers. "Next time, we're taking proper care of your friend. You got that?"

"Why don't you leave me alone?"

He steps past me, like I'm roadkill.

The cafeteria is more silent than a graveyard. Everyone's looking.

But worse.

Pinedale High's no cell phone policy is being fully ignored.

They're filming.

They're filming *me*.

I scratch up the remains of my lunch, dump it, and retreat to the bathroom.

Chapter 21

Two plus two equals five

Humiliation and shame sit thick and heavy. They weigh me down, pinning me to the floor.

I can't go back out there. All those students watching me, looking at me, laughing, pointing, filming.

I'll be all over the message apps.

Chopped up into memes or gifs.

Bite-size content.

It stings.

I'm in one of the stalls, sitting on the closed toilet seat. Girls have shuffled in, flushed and shuffled out again, chatted, done their make-up, brushed their hair, spilled the tea, and here I stay.

A tap's drip drip dripping. Every second and a half...*boop, boop, boop.*

The bell rang a loooong time ago.

Obvs, I can't stay in here all day. But why not? It's quiet, it's safe, and there are no bullies.

The stall door's locked. Though there are these weird gaps on the sides so everyone can see you doing your business. Haven't they heard about doors that run to the edges?

Yet another tale of the unexplained to add to my Pinedale High list.

Top of that list are the Bruno brothers and their little

mate, Evan.

What am I missing? Why does no one say anything against those guys? Are they funding the place? Are their fathers on the local police force? The town mayor? President?

Not even one person will stand up to them – are they that untouchable?

The whole thing's sus.

Why? Just why?

I don't get it.

My own kind? I'm sitting by myself. Even at Photography Club, I'm by myself. Who are they talking about?

I'd better get to class.

I might be branded as the *new kid,* but that doesn't mean I don't have to follow the rules.

I'd better get back out there. The last thing I need is detention. Visions of my father losing it are enough to spur me out of my pity party for one.

Besides, it's been a while since anyone used the facilities.

I unbolt the door, step out, and cry at my crime scene of a top reflected in the mirror. Even the jacket buttoned up tight can't disguise the extra splotches. I rinse what I can, fix my hair, wash my face.

Pull myself toward myself.

The hallway's quiet save for the janitor, who's mopping the floors. His name badge reads "Hank". He's older than mountains.

Will he rat me out? Lurking in the hallways during class time?

"Sorry about the behavior of those boys," he says. "They're no good."

My spirit slips lower. "You saw that?"

"The whole thing." He shakes his head. "Those brothers never did learn any manners. Need some discipline to keep them in line."

I couldn't disagree. "But they're allowed to get away with it."

"Some will argue it's kids, boys being boys, but sometimes you can see the adult they'll be, and it's worse." He rests on his broom like he's seen an eternity of students. He probably has. "I don't understand the kids of today."

Oh, here he goes. How we're flaky or have no idea about anything or are attached to our phones or are too woke or are too dependent on our parents or are snowflakes and about a hundred or so other generalizations.

"It's the thing to rebel. I get it. It's fashionable, and all kids do it. But what's wrong with getting good grades, getting a good job, and starting a family…settling down to the business of living." He's hit his stride now. "Anyone who lived through the '29 crash knows that."

Say what? "The '29 crash?"

"You were lucky to have a roof over your head and a hot meal in your belly," he explains with a dead serious expression.

I don't know what he's talking about. '29 crash? What *is* that?

"Yeah, I guess so." A brief memory of a history class flickers into my consciousness. "Do you mean the Great Depression?"

"Is there another?"

Depression's taken on another meaning since then. Nearly everyone I know is in some kind of great depression, but this guy's talking about something that happened nearly a hundred years ago like it's yesterday.

Is everyone in this place stuck in the past?

"Kids of today don't know how easy they've got it," he says. "To have that choice. Maybe it's because they have the choice that they don't know how important it is."

I half-grasp what he's saying. "That to fight to have the right is more difficult than to have the right?"

"Exactly."

I kind of get it. Mom used to say that if she were my age, it wouldn't be a big deal. Mental health is a thing now. Back then, it wasn't. If you had challenges, you could be committed. Even if it wasn't that serious, you could find yourself in a sanatorium, like Mom.

We had mental-wellness days at my old school. They'd talk about anxiety and depression like they were old mates who occasionally pulled up at your home when you hadn't got your shit together for a few weeks to sit with you in the dark.

"Those boys are lucky they won't be sent off to Korea." Hank takes his cap off, runs his hand through his hair, and tugs the cap back on again. "Though the military might help sort them out."

And I'm back in mad world again. Korea? Sent to Korea? Is this another expression like "having a cow"? You're "sent to Korea"?

"Yes, sir," I say. "The military is an option."

He shakes his head. "It's never an option. We lost some brave men in the war." He seems to drift away on a cloud of memory. Lost some brave men in the war? Which war? There've been plenty. He sounds like my grandfather when he used to talk about growing up with rationing. But, of course, my grandfather meant World War II.

Not unless...don't be ridiculous. That would make Hank...I tried to do the math in my head...about ninety. He was ancient but not entirely decrepit. How many ninety-year-olds were working as janitors? To be fair, he was closer to my dad's age, so not about to shuffle off his mortal coil anytime soon.

The great fire of '53. That's what Joe had said.

Two and two were adding together and making five.

Unless...but that was impossible.

Definitely impossible.

A sick feeling turns over my stomach and shakes it empty.

Just because it sounds illogical doesn't mean that it's not the logical explanation.

It was the simplest.

But that means—

Hank clears his throat. "Aren't you supposed to be in class, little lady?"

There's a soft tease in his voice, and I know he'd never rat me out. "Heading there now."

My thoughts toss, turn, and tumble.

Behind me, Hank's back to mopping, sloshing the water in the bucket. It clanks as the mop hits the sides. He's lathering it up good and proper, swilling out the dirt. Then he plops the mop onto the tiles, wiping it back and forth like he's done it a hundred thousand times, maybe more. Which he probably has.

There's one problem.

And I can't unsee it.

It must be a trick of the eye. The tilt of my head. The position of the light.

No matter how much he's mopping and pushing and sloshing.

The floor's not wet.

Chapter 22

Click

My mother said she was eight when it first happened.

She'd been waiting for the school bus outside her parents' house.

They lived in this remote part of the Welsh countryside. Lots of sheep. Lots of moody grey skies.

An only child, my mom was used to "asking the expert", which is how she described talking to herself.

You could hear her muttering away from the other side of the house. A whole conversation sometimes, too.

She'd wait for the bus, listing the chores she had to do that day out loud. Sometimes, she'd sing too. Not in tune but a good belting from deep in her lungs.

The only thing that responded were the sheep. And even they weren't consistent. An occasional bleh-bleh here and a bleh-bleh there.

Imagine her surprise when one day, on finding a five-pound note lying on the road between the farm gate and the pathway that led back to her parents' house, she also found a boy about her age, a rucksack on his back and a folded map in his hand.

Five pounds was a king's ransom back then. She'd picked it up and immediately searched for the possible owner.

The empty fields called back to her, lonely as ever.

"Should I keep it, or should I turn it in?" A moral dilemma for the ages. "Finders keepers, yes. But it doesn't belong to me—"

The note in her hand represented so many possibilities. Sweets for days from the post office. A new saddle for her bike. Comic books, loads and loads of comic books. Do the right thing.

Amazing what one piece of printed paper could do.

"What if I kept it and didn't tell anyone? Just kept it safe and if no one reported it missing, I could use it then?"

She didn't expect an answer.

"You could give it me, and I'd press it to good use."

My mom said she nearly dove straight out of her skin when she heard that voice. Where he'd come from, she had no idea. There'd been no one and nothing to see for miles. Then, all of a sudden, there he was. Right in front of her.

Peter Jackson.

He was about the same age as her and determined. His chin jutted, his forehead high, and his entire manner intent on his purpose. Which, as it turned out, was to run away from home.

This fascinated my mother more than anything in the world.

She'd imagined getting onto a bus and disappearing on an adventure numerous times and had only got as far as the garden gate. Well, maybe down by the cliffs, but the sea made farther passage impossible.

And now here was someone actually following through.

She was awestruck. Five whole pounds and a literal

god amongst very young men...okay, boys. On the same morning.

He showed her his flask—*thermos*— his proposed bus route, and his shell collection, which he kept in a rusted tin with soldiers on the front.

"So you're going ahead with it?"

He nodded, tucking his map back into his pocket. "There's no backing out now. My cousins live in London, so I'll stop in there first before making my next move."

"Where to?"

"Africa."

Africa. Beyond my mother's wildest imaginings. "What will you do when you get there?"

"Lion taming."

Well, this was it for my mother. She absolutely, positively had to support her new friend's thriving ambition to charter the wild seas and explore the plains of Africa. It was so...*romantic*. Not that she knew what that meant, but as she put it to me, and believe me, she told me this story many, many times: "There was a certain impractical, starry-eyedness to the whole concept that had me drifting into dreamland."

"You have to take the five pounds." She handed him the money. "Take it and send me a postcard when you get to Africa."

Around this time, my grandmother called for my mother. An unusual occurrence. My mother also couldn't help but notice that the bus, usually punctual in the extreme, was decidedly late.

"You have to go in?" asked Peter. "I had hoped you'd wait with me. For the bus."

"I'll hurry back," she promised.

My grandmother waited at the front door. "The bus won't be coming past today. There's been an accident."

"Does this mean no school?" Hope sprang eternal.

"I'll run you up there." No such luck.

"Can you give Peter a lift too? He's also waiting for the bus."

"Is that who you were talking to out there? It's the first time you've given them a name."

"Who a name?"

Apparently, my grandmother looked awkward. "Yes, I'll give you both a lift."

"I'm not talking to myself this time. He's out there, look."

But you know, and I know, Peter wasn't there.

He'd been killed earlier that morning.

My mother found that out a few days later when it was in the papers. A memorial for Peter Jackson, who'd been killed on 8 November 1983. Hit by the school bus. He'd been reaching over to pick something up from the road and the driver hadn't seen him in time to brake.

It was then that my mother remembered the five-pound note.

Peter's life for a whole five pounds.

"The problem is, Lila, I can't tell who's living and who's dead. They look all the same to me. But to other people…"

They thought she was nuts. Crazy. Mad. Talking to dead people?

Her official diagnosis was paranoid schizophrenic.

Seeing things that aren't there.

Like ghosts.

Ghosts don't exist, right?

But to my mother, they do. They did.

They'd talk to her like I'd talk to you. It was only the details that would indicate something else was going on. The untouched meals. The tendency to wear the same clothes. The lack of water in the bucket...

"I have to be so careful, Lila. What will people think if they knew?"

A mental health disorder diagnosis and a loony bin. That's what.

I'll tell you a secret, I loved that story of Peter Jackson.

A *ghost*. She was talking to a *ghost*? There was something thrilling and scary and horrifying about it. I was the one who made her tell that story over and over again, even when I stopped believing it was true.

It was a great story. But it was a story.

A made-up tale to cover over the reality.

She suffered from severe mental illness.

There is no such thing as ghosts.

I'm not going mad.

There. I've said it out loud.

I'm not.

But...but...but.

Fuzzwhat greets me, and I sort out her food, the litter tray, and load her up with cuddles. She knows I'm not crazy.

I'm just the human who rescued her from outside and a life spent foraging in the rubbish.

Yes, she knows I'm not disclosing her presence. Which is lying-ish.

But I am not insane.

I am not my mother.

I open up my phone, search for Pinedale High, and scroll through their website.

About Us. Blah, blah, blah.

History. Blah, blah, blah.

Gallery.

Paydirt.

Pinedale in the '60s, the '70s, the '80s.

The '50s.

And there's the proof I was dreading.

A photo of the Bruno brothers and their bikes in the foreground of a shot of the school. Black and white. 1953, the date stamp.

Things click into place.

That's what the dreams were – it was how they died.

The Bruno Brothers and Evan in a fire.

Sam, chased and hounded by bullies.

Ghosts.

They're ghosts.

Chapter 23

Going viral

The truth squats over me.

A giant belching toad.

There's no way the socials didn't blow up. I couldn't miss with my lunchtime *performance*.

Me yelling at thin air.

Talking to myself.

Threatening Mr. Invisible.

Tripping is one thing, heading into an inexplicable rant is another.

They must think I'm a complete loser.

Crazy.

Nuts.

Mad.

Just like my mom.

She used to have entire conversations with blank space. Laughing, joking, animated. Like she was talking to someone else. My grandmother said it was her imaginary friends, and she didn't grow out of it like she was supposed to.

Mom said it was people who had died who still had business on this plane. Though that explanation bobbed and weaved.

Right before she died, she muttered that it was spirits who didn't want to let go. They couldn't. The hold to the living was tightfast. Nothing to do with unfinished business. Or catching their killers. Or some sort of revenge.

Peter Jackson, armed with his map and his five whole pounds, thought he was still alive, waiting for a bus that would never arrive.

Mom said she did see him a few times after that. Always a variation on the same theme. He was running away to Antarctica. He was on a mission to infiltrate the Soviet government. He'd had a fight with his dad. That one made her cry, she'd said. Because even his ghost self had stopped pretending he was someone else.

Then, one day, Peter simply disappeared.

Into the ether.

Gone.

My insides feel hollowed out. How can this be happening to me? Was it genetic? Passed on through the bloodlines?

Are these ghosts really there, though?

How can I be sure it's not my brain making this whole thing up? Creating people who don't exist? That's how paranoia works, you know.

Whispers, visions, all from faulty brain networking. Some people convince themselves they're a superhero and fall off their roofs. Others think they're some sort of god sent down with a celestial message. And there are others who are resolute that they're being pursued by the CIA, the FBI, the men in white, the little grey men, or the men with blue hands. To steal their garden gnome collection the second their back's turned.

That's what the doctors told my mother (not about the gnomes).

Her brain simply misfired.

It doesn't align with reality.

It happens.

And there's medication to treat.

My mother never accepted that explanation, though. Fought against it. But how do you explain that to people who can't see, can't hear, or can't feel it? You sound...crazy. Ah. I'm back there again.

She used to say that people prayed to God, which was talking to a being you can't see or hear. And that was all just fine. But ghosts?

There's no such thing.

Period.

Fuzzwhat's stretched alongside me, her tiny kitty belly all round and soft. Is she real? I put my hand on her, and she makes that *prrr* chirp they do when they're sleeping and you disturb them. So adorbs.

She's real because if I'm here, she's here. She doesn't fade in and fade out.

I'm talking to myself to reassure myself that I still have a strong hold on reality. This could be a simple temporary blip. A stress response to the past few months, which have been awful, with a side helping of utterly dreadful.

There's a glitch in my system.

That's all.

Bits and pieces of conversation with my mother shuffle to the surface. Things like: Be careful of angry ghosts because they can push objects, people, even. I have the stained shirt to prove this. She also said that they sometimes thought she was dead too. Because she could see them.

Why didn't I listen?

Why wasn't I paying attention?

Because I was embarrassed, ashamed, even? Why couldn't she be like Jo's mother, who jogged and read thick novels and whinged about the price of a good plumber? There was no talk of removing parts of Jo's mother's brain, or locking her up for her own good, or taking away her freedom.

I swallow back the rising tide of fear.

This can't end well. I'm just like her. And look how warm and fuzzy society was with her.

I want to phone my grandmother right now. The urge is real. She's in a retirement home and has Alzheimer's, so the chances are high she won't remember me, or she'll think I'm Mom. I might get lucky, though. Catch her in that fleeting moment where her voice softens and embraces me from a thousand miles away.

"Eccentric" is what she called my mom. She loved her. Even if she spent her time talking to herself.

My Nan's not on the messaging app, though.

And my phone doesn't have roaming.

I text Jo.

—*Hey, babe! Pinedale's sitting on the hellmouth. Send me the latest tea!*—

Oh man, the time difference. She's ahead, behind? Ahead seven hours.

My text sits on delivered.

A new start. A clean slate. Dad's words.

Empty.

Grace? Ah, but is she a ghost or an actual human?

I park that idea.

Why here? Why now? What did Joe say? With Pinedale, you never know. Or something like that? What did that mean? Is Pinedale a walking graveyard?

The only person who can answer my questions is gone.

I fire up my doomscrolling. They've re-released an iconic discontinued frosted lipstick. The influencer MA swatches on the back of her hand, careful not to damage her vintage lipstick, to check. Is it a dupe? Or have they changed the formula?

Good question.

With every iteration, there are modifications. Ha! Turns out there's no mica or silica in this particular re-release. Makes it greasier, less matte. As the influencer points out, "Everything is yellower nowadays."

How true.

This particular brand is still way out of my price bracket.

The next video is of a conversation with the universe.

Shots fired with every question.

It's relatable.

I remember sitting with Jo this time last year, talking about our first year of high school. The good, the bad, the downright fugly. I'd said, "Hey, maybe this year will be better?"

And the universe responded, "Is it?"

Shots fired.

Two days later, Mom had "that" episode.

Fuzzwhat's eye is definitely worse. It's stuck closed. And crusty.

I scroll to the next video.

The latest dance. Over and over and over. I like the song, so repeat, repeat, repeat doesn't bother me. It will be stuck in my head for days, and that's okay. There's a space for noisy, repetitive stuff. And talking to ghosts, it seems.

Some people get to be good at math, and others get to have extra-sensory perception.

One more video.

One more.

Just…

One…

More.

Chapter 24

Into the woods…again

Ah! I ease into my happy place.

It's the sharp freshness, the quiet, the whispering of the plants and trees—there's nothing better.

Nothing but calm.

There's no hurry to get somewhere on time, no pressure to perform, to go, go, go—always at 100%, no half-assing, 'cos who half-asses shit? Only losers, right? Keep moving, pushing, winning, winning, winning. 'Cos, again, no one wants to be a loser, only there's always a loser if there's a winner.

Zero-sum game.

That's what sports teaches.

Win.

Win against all costs.

Win against all odds.

Push. Keep going.

It's…exhausting.

It's noisy.

There's no there, *there*. It's always about the next thing. Strive, push, win, repeat.

But I'm here now.

Unshackled. At ease. Slow.

So much isn't said about slow.

The amble, the going nowhere slowly of

nothingness that's way more than the agony of busyness.

I could do this forever.

This. This is me.

There's a sense of connection that convinces me that whatever celestial being might be out there is one with this. Nature. The land. The animals. The water. All of it. Connected. A perfect network of symbiotic rhythm. Oneness. A divine communion with green. You could argue that man doesn't belong here. The master and commander of their environment. I disagree.

We are part of it.

All of it.

We're so intent on destroying it, we don't realize we're slowly un-aliving ourselves. Look at me. *Un-aliving.*

A bird calls, and insects are humming, the soft rustle of movement unseen, but it's there, an entire world beneath my feet.

It's humbling,

There is so much we have to learn from them.

There's the south path that's slowly grown over. You can't get a truck down here, not without removing most of the trees. So it's been left untouched. They also put a series of warnings out at the school.

There were rumors about a kid getting lost out here. But that was a long time ago. I know what I'm doing. I've been in and out of these woods for years, since I was five. My father took me on my first trip out here. To shoot deer.

A rite of passage, he called it.

I couldn't do it.

Those eyes looking back at me, the soft tha-thump of her heart in her chest. And for what? To be stuffed and hung on a wall? He handed me the gun that was almost twice my height, put my finger on the trigger, and told me to pull. I recoiled before I pulled. The doe fled. My heart was full.

That one. I could make a difference to that one.

Some day in the future, I'll help all of them.

My father still takes my brothers out here.

I make sure I'm busy with something else.

Anything else.

This is deeper into the south side than I've gone before. A carpet of ferns unfurls. Magnificent ferns. The sun catches them just so, and their fingers move as if they're signing to each other. Maybe they are.

Who are we to say they aren't?

There's so much we don't know.

There's a theory that megalodon still cruises the deep sea. How would we know? So how would we know what's really in these forests?

Animals aren't stupid. They're intelligent, and they have intelligence. They know to stay far away from us.

To go left? Or right?

The path less travelled?

Absolutely.

Why is that even a question?

I take a swig from my water bottle. It's thirsty work, exploring. It's cool, though I'm only going to be an hour or so, and then I'll head back. Homework calls.

The ground slopes down into a rocky ravine. If I head that way, there's rock climbing in my future for sure. Stones turn to rocks, turn to boulders. Some look like giant faces.

My hiking shoes can comfortably make the journey.

The call to adventure is too strong.

The thing about rock climbing is that you spend so much time focusing on your next step that, before you know it, you're miles ahead of where you should be. When I look up to check on my surroundings, the first beat of panic sounds in my chest. Nothing looks familiar.

It's okay. I can follow my path back.

There's always a solution, as my father says. And if you can't find a solution, you're not looking hard enough. Actually, he says, "You're the problem."

A hint of emotion propels me forward. I can do this.

I climb back the way I came, but there's one problem.

I can't find the path.

There are no ferns.

Somehow, I've put myself in an entirely different position from the one I started in.

If I climb farther east, there's what looks like a rocky outcrop. Potentially a ledge. That will give me the vantage point I need to logic my way through this.

I make my way toward it and scale the rock face with a few moves.

From the edge, there are mostly treetops, but look what I found—there's also a rock pool.

A secret swimming pool. This is awesome.

Any panic slides away, and in its place is pure excitement. I can come out here, swim, and enjoy a total vacation from everything and everyone.

I'm so excited about future me's plans, I don't see the gap until it's too late.

One moment, there's solid ground. The next, I'm falling. Not too far. But enough to hit something jagged hard.

The wind is immediately sucked from my lungs. My

brain takes a second to catch up to what's happened. A cave? There's a sliver of light above me where I fell. Then the pain rushes in, all at once.

I want to die. It's solid, rushing agony. All of my attention focuses on my shin, that's snapped in half.

Any movement feels like red-hot pokers on my skin. It's okay. I can get out of here. Ignoring the screaming from my leg, I hoist myself up on my arms, push my palms into the grit. The pain zigzags up me, threatening to knock me unconscious. My God, unconscious would be better right now.

I can't see that well. It's broken, right? I've broken it?

My mouth's so dry, I could down a fountain of water. The rock pool. It was so close. And how am I getting out of here to head there?

I have to get out of here.

There's no cell reception. I try anyway, but even with my newly cracked screen, the lack of bars tells me I won't be calling anyone to help.

Sounds like a you problem.

Jesus, if my dad could not be in the cave with me right now.

He's right, though. It *is* a me problem.

This means there must be a me solution.

An ant's nipping my ankle.

If I don't think of a way out, I'm ending up as worm food.

Worm food. Fish food. Bear food. Fern food. Food fern. Burn. Red burn. Red fern.

Someone hands me a telephone, and it rings VERY LOUDLY.

Like a phone alarm.

My eyes stagger open. What a peculiar dream. I hit snooze and sink back onto my pillow.

Who was that, even? I'm going with the student who went into the woods who they couldn't find. That doesn't fit, though. It's like stuffing a puzzle piece into position. My heart sinks. It must be someone I've met at school. A dead someone. A ghost.

This is how they died.

And their body is rotting in a cave somewhere near a rock pool. Poor guy.

So much for his happy place.

If I didn't know better, it felt like Joe.

But Joe's not dead.

Is he?

Chapter 25

What's reality anyway?

Today would be a good day to have a buddy waiting for me at the top of the stairs.

But Joe's not here. My spirits sink. Bad-tempered, impatient or not, he might buffer me from the stares, the pointing, the laughing.

Always, some jackass has to laugh.

I get it. It's relief that it's not them.

They didn't fall into their lunch tray in front of everyone and then start tearing a strip off Mr. Nobody and his mates.

At least, that's what I'm telling myself.

My outfit is completely incorrect.

I'm wearing a jumpsuit that I was convinced was cute.

It screams, "You're trying too hard, and you need to give up."

A girl with orange corkscrew curls sniggers and mutters something under her breath. I can't quite catch it. Was she referring to me?

A guy with a cap pulled on backward pulls the same move. Only he's not so subtle. "Lady Cringe".

That's what I've been christened.

And it's said in what I can only call a *posh* accent. One of those upper-crust, super-snobby, vowel-enunciating accents that's definitely not me. All la-di-da and uppity.

"You fancy a shag, Lady Cringe?" yells some bozo with no imagination from the parking lot.

"Stop it! Stop it! You're all so mean!" mocks a girl with long dark hair and a sports-team sweater. "Sooooooo mean, look what you did. You horrible people."

I mean, I didn't say that.

My face is pure flames. My neck is on fire too. My ears are moments from self-combusting.

I want to die. Really die. Crawl up into a ball, tight and snug, and let death take me away.

A squeaky-voiced girl's revved up the chanting. "Lady Cringe, Lady Cringe, Lady Cringe."

Although they can't keep the accent and the rhythm. Like rubbing your belly and your head at the same time.

I wish I was one of those people who could turn around, bravely face my taunters, and say, "I give you a nine out of ten for effort, but it's a no from me in terms of execution."

But if I open my mouth, my teeth will fall out instead.

They're following me.

I can't remember where to go. Which way is Math? Or is it History? English. It's English. Of course it's English. Start the day off with your own fan club and then an onslaught of past and present participles.

I keep my head down. Wrong move. It's all feet everywhere I look.

An arm links in mine and yanks me into a classroom.

I freeze. It's Evan, my slick, greased-up bully of a boy. "We really need to talk."

So many conflicting thoughts assault me.

He can move objects…*people*!

His skin is acne scarred, every pore a crater. It has depth. Gravitas. Flesh.

His voice is bold. Not throaty, or whispery, or groany like some haunted house actor's.

And yet, he's dead.

Deadity dead.

Gone from this earth.

His hand grips my arm, and there's real strength behind it. How? Am I hallucinating? "The night of the fire…"

I wrestle away from him back into the stream of students.

And goodie, some have been waiting for me. "Lady Cringe! How's the taste of floor ass?"

"Hey, loser, next time try eating at the table. Works for me!"

"Bet you think you're so great now, right?"

This time next week, it'll be someone else's turn. That's worse though, isn't it? Wishing it on some complete random stranger.

I duck down corridor after corridor, hoping one will look familiar.

There's Grace!

She's stretching out a leg muscle by pushing on a locker. Or she's trying to push the locker into the wall. I can't tell.

"Hey, G—"

I stop. What if she's…one of them?

No, she gave me those plastic bags. Did she, though? Or were there bags on the table and I took them? Did she physically hand them to me? But wait, the Bruno brothers, Evan, they can move things. They tripped up Joe.

And I swear Evan's thumbprints are wrapped round my upper arm.

Why would she be holding plastic bags?

I risk it. "Grace!"

"Hey, how are you holding up? Seems there are some really mean people here." She says it pointedly, glaring at some of my unofficial fan club. "What? You never tripped up? Had a bad day?"

I'm not sure if that's better or worse. Probably worse.

One or two have the decency to look embarrassed. Another is defiant. Who is Grace to spoil his fun? Loser. Jerk. *Creep.* I dread to think what the comments section looks like, if this is the real-life reception.

"Thanks, it's been…rough."

"There's a spare seat next to me." She shepherds me into English class. "I'll make sure they don't bite you."

Please, please, please let her be real. The mortification if I'm wrong.

"Grace Hanratty, if you could please hand out today's readers," says the English teacher whose name I've completely forgotten. Although she looks like the walking dead, she isn't. They wouldn't hire a ghost teacher. That would be weird.

My shoulders relax, and my breathing loosens up. All this tension is not good for me.

I take the seat next to Grace.

She beetles off to hand out texts.

The class is full. Every seat accounted for. But there was a spare next to Grace. Therefore, by the process of logical deduction to an illogical and yet logical explanation—there's a ghost riding along in English class.

But who?

The teacher's droning on. Everyone's unfamiliar to me. That's what you get for being the new kid.

There's a guy who likes to smack gum, another who draws with pen and ink on paper, and another who wears his hair in a mohawk. Could it be one of them? Likely suspects include rule breakers. It's not like they'd get caught. Gum smacker is high on my list for ectoplasmic explanation.

A girl with serious mouth jewelry gazes out the window. Another has her head on the desk while she texts on her lap.

1953 would be when Evan died. That's a long time to keep coming to school. What does he do during vacation? Or do they have a different idea of time?

I bet it's that girl there with the metal band T-shirt and dog collar. No one wears those anymore. Wait, hang on. Jo's much older sister had one. Last year. By much older, I mean 18.

Scratch that. It's not her.

What's fashionable Londonside might only be fashionable now or vice versa.

How do I tell?

Mom, if you can hear me, how do I know who's living and who's dead?

I could really use the intel about now.

It's probably that shy guy who sits in the back, keeping to himself and his worm collection. Or the girl who says mean things to complete strangers' backs because she saw them on the socials. Would a ghost still be able to read? Or to watch videos?

My thoughts check back to Evan.

He surely knows that he and his compadres bit it in the fire?

Maybe he doesn't.

No, he knows. There's a solid "yes" in my gut.

From where I don't know.

So what gives?

It would be so much easier if ghosts were green and floated. Or if you could see straight through them.

He. Gripped. My. Arm.

I could be in real trouble here.

Chapter 26

Sam's a ghost?

Lunch looms like a specter. If you'll pardon the expression.

Gathering up courage is tiring. I can't be asked. My stomach's grumbling worse than an angry bear.

I grab a bag of potato chips and an apple to snack on and haul my butt back out before they spot me and start up the chants again.

Eat it up.

Cringe queen.

Lo-ser.

Where are my big-girl panties? In a crate somewhere over the Atlantic. I wouldn't mind being them right now, all tucked up and safe in a wooden box. No need to make a public appearance anytime soon. Or ever.

Do I want to eat lunch in the bathroom? No.

But the bathroom it has to be.

This time, I have no problem finding the senior girls' bathroom.

When I see Sam in their usual place in front of the mirror, I could cry. Great big, snotty sobs of relief.

They're drawing hearts and lightning bolts on their cheeks with green eyeliner. "Hey, hon? What happened to you? You look like roadkill."

"Way to soften the blow." I keep my voice nice and even stevens, but there's no doubt, it's the same outfit. The stirrup pants. The dayglo. The pom-poms. How had I not noticed before? Oh, there was an overall. That's why.

A few other puzzle pieces click into place.

The bangs that wouldn't turn blue. The lipstick that wouldn't stain black.

Turns out you *do* have an eternity outfit.

Suddenly, I don't know what to say. How are you doing? What's up?

Sam grabs the awkward by the thorns. "Whatever it is you want to say, say it!"

Talk about reading my mind. "I...well...was thinking about how things don't turn out the way you planned. Or how I planned. I thought coming here would be this whole new slate, a new opportunity to, I don't know, be someone different. No, what am I saying? Not be someone different. But start again."

"It's teething pains. Everyone gets them. Sometimes, to be the person you are, you have to shed the person you've become. Look at me. It's a risk, but it's the eighties. Times are changing."

Ooo-kaaay. "Yeah, that's true."

"And you're a sassy Londoner, ain't ya? I'd die to be brought up in a big city like that. You're already way cooler than you realize." They pause. "Are those kids giving you a hard time?"

I nod.

They sigh. "It'll get better." They half-mean it too.

A sadness reaches deep into my soul. That dream. Out in the woods. Those bullies didn't let up until—"Are those kids giving *you* a hard time?"

Sam glances at me, then looks away. "What have you been hearing?" There's a sharpness in their voice. "Don't worry about me. I'm old enough and ugly enough to look after myself." They draw a heart with an arrow through it on their cheek. "Besides, this is our safe space. No one can touch us in here."

The bathroom. Hiding. In the bathroom.

An eternity in a senior girls' bathroom.

A loud bang jolts us both. A car backfiring maybe?

We exchange a glance.

I peer into the corridor. Very slowleee. I've read enough about American schools. A very real fear prickles.

A locker lies on its side. A few gym bros take turns in lifting it, showing off to each other. Lame.

"Nothing to worry about—"

Sam looks like they've seen, well, a ghost. "Is he out there?"

"Wh-who?"

They can barely get his name out. "Chad."

"Who's Chad?"

"*Who's Chad*? Do you live under a rock, girl? Who's Chad?" Sam recovers her usual swagger and style. "Only the Pinedale High golden boy. You'd think he shits the stuff, the way they all applaud for him." Their hand shakes as they return to green hearts. "Chad and his friends rule Pinedale. No one says or does anything without his say-so. Just steer clear. The year's 1987, and you'd swear it was the fifties, they're so straight."

I sit on the question I want to ask. What car does he drive? Is it sleek, white, and fast? With the top down?

"Chad and his friends don't understand people like you and me, that's all." There's a waver to their voice.

"Are you scared?"

"It doesn't help to be scared. You have to stand up to his kind, or they'll walk all over you." They give me a weak smile. "Don't get on the wrong side of him when he's with his mate, Chaz. Now he's plain psycho. If you told me he killed his pet cat for fun as a kid, I'd believe you."

"What does the school say?"

"The school?" They laugh. "Ha. Ha. Ha. Nothing. Why would you go against your star quarterback? He's supposed to be some big national shoo-in or whatever. Football boys are gods here. They'll carry him on their shoulders and give him a parade."

"Nothing changes then. That's depressing."

"It's the same over in Londontown?"

"Yeah, sure." I was thinking of Joe. Everyone loves Joe. He's not too bad, I guess. Grumpy. Is he dead? He wears that same jacket and jeans every day. The shirt might change, but I haven't seen it. Nah. He was talking to Grace. "Football stars rock."

"Right on. I don't see the big deal, catching and throwing a blown-up ball of pig leather. Whatever blows your hair back."

My brain's still processing the information, sifting it through. "1987."

"Right? They banned Boy George from a TV show for being a bad influence. Can you believe?"

I have no idea who that is. "Scandal."

"Things will be different as soon as I get to New York."

There's a giant lump in my throat. They never get to

New York. They're here, for all eternity. In this bathroom.

"Could you check for me?" Sam fluffs out their hair. "If he's out there? I promised my mom I'd be home early, skip woodwork." Their hand drops to their wrist, searches for something, and for the smallest moment, there's a look of anguish on their face.

The ribbon. Sam's looking for the ribbon their mother gave them.

They died without it.

A rush of nausea overwhelms me. I fight back the tears that arrive fierce and sudden. "I'll have a look for you."

I go through the motions. Of course, Chad's not here. He and his mate, Chaz, ran my friend off the road thirty-something years ago and killed them. Was he caught? Did anyone arrest him, prosecute him, even? Or has he gone on to whatever life the golden boy of Pinedale High had waiting for him?

"All clear," I say in an unnaturally high voice. "The corridor's devoid of life, human or otherwise."

"You say very strange things, you know." They take another moment to straighten their top. "I'll be out in a moment."

The end of lunch signals. I exit the bathroom and bump straight into Grace.

"Hey, stranger, cheer squad was cancelled, so I was looking for you everywhere. We don't use that bathroom, it's—"

"For seniors, I know."

Grace laughs. "*Anyone* can use it. I was going to say 'haunted'." She shivers. "C'mon, let's work together on that history project."

Chapter 27

When's a photo not a photo?

I open the shed door and Brian, Tomas, and Zook look at me in perfect synchronized motion, then pivot. The three of them sit alongside each other on straight-back chairs, their attention on the photo tacked to the wall. My photo. The one with my phantom greaser.

"Sorry, I'm late, I had to…" The door doesn't close behind me, and fifteen million minutes go by as I heave the door to. "Did I miss anything?"

Tomas tilts his head, his thumb rubbing against his chin. "We're considering the subject matter of your shot."

"That's not the one I wanted to submit." I could have sworn I chose the students-being-students candid shot, but no. "So yes, there's…this one."

"Hmmm," says Brian.

There's no chair for me. My hands search for something to do—play with my hair, splay my fingers, hide in my pockets. The developing table seems a viable option, but with these three, the mere thought of a bum, sorry, *butt*, touching their precious workspace will probably send them over the existential edge.

Evan's portrait appears as menacing as ever. The direct challenging gaze, the pointing arms, the do-you-dare stance.

Zook doesn't tear his eyes from my photo. "What made you choose this print?"

"There were some shadows, light…interesting shapes…and there's a history there. The old building. A fire….um. I don't know. The way the pieces all jiggle together." I'm clutching at paper straws in a hurricane here. "It's part of the school's heritage…I wanted to capture that essence…"

Tomas alights from his chair and peers closer. "That's an excellent way to describe it."

It is? I'm spitballing here. Pure freewheeling off a cliff.

"There's definitely a sense of otherworldliness." Zook places his hands behind his head and tilts his chair on the back two legs. "I would say nostalgia but certainly also a *je ne sais quoi.*"

"I take it you were running some experiments with the aperture?" Brian vaguely glances in my direction. "Or, of course, you might have overexposed your film and ended up with a happy accident."

Happy accident? Overexposure? Aperture?

He throws up his hands. "It works, though. Gotta give you that."

"Beginner's luck's what I call it," announces Tomas.

The other two nod.

"Impressive, though. I have to say I've tried, and I haven't been able to capture the elusive Pinedale Swish." Brian sighs. "And first go, Little Miss English hits pay dirt. Am I jealous? I'm above such emotions."

Are they looking at the same photo I am? What have I missed?

It's Evan standing in front of a building. Won't it be embarrassing if his name isn't Evan, and here I am calling him that on the flimsy evidence of a dream, well, more a nightmare.

No, no, that *is* his name. Evan. I can't describe it. It's a knowing. A surety that won't budge. Ah! It's probably my intuition, that most maligned and misunderstood "thing" that I frequently ignore to my detriment.

Yeah, that's Evan. Evan... *Reynolds.*

I pause.

"I asked, did you know that this was a Pinedale High anomaly? Something to do with the geography or the climate, I don't know." Brian's voice fades in, like a slide animation. "There were some scientists, photographers who came to study the phenomenon, and that's the explanation they gave, pretty flimsy if you ask me."

"Nah, they said it was the curve of the planet and the effect of the woods," corrects Zook. "I don't believe that, though. It's probably overexposed film. I mean, newbie here gets it on her first shot."

There's definitely equal amounts envy and amazement in his voice.

"As you said, beginner's luck," I say. "I don't know how he got in the shot, but when I developed the film, there he was."

Oh, and there it is again. The is-that-girl-crazy? look.

"We're talking about the blur," explains Tomas, once more heading for a close-up inspection. "Perfect, dead center, an excellent example of its kind."

"The blur?" There's no blur that I can see.

"That's what we call it. Affectionately. The blur. It's the swish. The Pinedale Swish. So named because it seems to happen here more than anywhere else."

"That we know of," interjects Brian.

"Admittedly," says Tomas, sounding like the professor he's bound to become, boring everyone with his big words and blah, blah, blah. "Like Brian said, it's an anomaly. We've been trying for years to capture it."

My brain is slow to catch up. "So it's not the guy you're talking about?"

"What guy?"

Oooooohhhhhh. *Ohhhh*. My heart rate quickens. In a good way. "There are other photos like this, you say?"

"Not many. Maybe thirty or so," says Tomas. "Over the past fifty or sixty years."

"You don't say?" Thirty. That's thirty ghosts hanging out in Pinedale High. Or the same few ghosts photobombing the photography clubs of old. "And it's a phenomenon specific to here?"

Zonk curls his lips down in an exaggerated grimace. "Seems so."

You know what this means? It's here, it's the school, it's not *me*. Well, it is me, but forget the senior girls' bathroom. The school is clearly *haunted* haunted, proper haunted. My sincere delight at this revelation has my three fellow shutterbugs completely confused. My condolences. Welcome to *my* club.

"How did you do it?" asks Tomas.

My mind's already racing. "Where can you see the other photos like this? Are they online? Is there a handle?"

"You can look it up," says Brian.

Zooks already has his phone out, tap-tap-tapping

away. "Here."

"The Pinedale High Swish. They could have thought of a better name." I take the phone from him and scroll. Pic after pic of people. If anything, they're unremarkable. To me. A woman in a hoop skirt waves. A student on a skateboard whizzes by. A group of girlfriends are playing jump rope.

"Sometimes it's a small blur, other times it's bigger," explains Zooks.

Depends on the number of ghosts. Obvs. If you didn't know it, you'd think it was a walk down Pinedale High's memory lane. Different hair, different fashions, different purses. The buildings move and change, too. Some in color, some without.

It's fascinating to me but for different reasons than Brian, Tomas, and Zooks.

"Red block, yellow block, blue block!" Like those multi-colored bricks you get, all stacked up on each other. "That must be how they did it in the '80s. Clever." And now it's Block 1, Block 2, Block 3. In grey.

Sam's not in any of the swish pictures. Or the Bruno Brothers.

"We can add yours to the collection if you like," says Zooks. "You'd have to give the date, the time, that kind of info to the officials. Tbh, it's kind of a pain in the butt."

"Sure." Ghosts photograph as swishes or blurs or splodges or wispy willows or overexposure. Got it.

"Welcome, officially, to the club," says Tomas. He gives a nod.

I nod back, cool, calm and collected. Something's gone right. It's a fluke, a chance, a complete accident.

I'll take it.

Chapter 28

Fuzzywhat

"Why's there a kitten in the house?"

I've been home less than ten seconds.

My father's eyes are squinty with exhaustion and bloodshot with yesterday's beer binge. He's holding Fuzzwhat in his hand, and she's wriggling and a-wiggling to escape, tiny kitten paws and claws in full warrior mode. "You said you would take it to the authorities."

Each word is clipped, almost as if he said them through gritted teeth. Warning. Danger. Do not proceed.

Things will not turn out... *well*.

"I'm sorry. I meant to, but with school—"

"How many times do I have to ask you? I don't want a cat in the house. They bring extra work, and someone has to feed it and take it to the vet. Do you expect me to do that?"

I stealth move around him, aiming for the stairs.

"You don't make decisions without my say-so, are we clear?"

"Yes."

"You will take this thing..."

Fuzz chooses this moment to free dive from his hand to the floor, a tiny fluffy missile.

"Goddamit, it scratched me." My father's

examining his thumb as though someone's blown it off with a shotgun. "I won't hear another word about this."

She runs straight to me, mewing her head off.

I scoop her up and tuck her close to me.

Any happiness I felt from my Pinedale swishy swish leaks out of me like a deflated balloon. "I'm sorry. I'll take her."

I'm about to swishy swish Fuzz upstairs, but no such luck.

"Wait. We need to talk about something."

He ushers me into the kitchen, still the only living space that's mostly furnished.

Fuzz rests on my shoulder, and I try to pretend she's not there.

My father grabs a beer from the fridge, cranks it open, and takes a sip that's half a can long. Then he pulls up a barstool and sits down with his full weight. "So, I got a call from a Mrs. Linton. She says she's your guidance counsellor?"

Oh, the eyelash lady. "I had to see her on my first day, some sort of protocol."

He nods. "How'd that go, by the way? The first day?"

"Great." Where's this going? And why do I sense it's up a certain creek without a paddle?

My father's stalling. He's taking another sip, turning the can, label front facing. If this were a coffee table, he'd put the can in the corner and only the corner. He's also adjusting and readjusting his watch strap. An old-timey watch, not a smart one.

"You'd tell me if anything happened?"

Now, there's a conversation starter.

He elaborates. "Anything like your mother."

There's a resounding crash in my brain. The cafeteria. The videos. My mouth is so dry it would rival a desert. "Sure, Dad."

He opens the clasp on his watch, then clicks it closed. "Mrs. Linton called me to say that she was…concerned."

I'm cornered. Father to the front of me, guidance counsellor to the right, social media mayhem behind me.

"Oh, yes, she asked me about what I wanted to study, and when I said I didn't know, she reminded me that I needed to start making choices about my future." Truth be told, I can't remember what she said to me. "Oh yes, and she signed me up for the photography club, and I've already had some success there. The guys told me I managed to capture—" Whoa! A *ghost.* I photoed a ghost. Mayday, mayday. "—the light really well."

"That's good." He's twisting the can again. "She mentioned that you were distracted by noises?"

"Noises? There were some kids goofing around, the usual."

There's a pained expression on his face. "Nothing…unusual?"

"No."

"She also said that you had some difficulties? That some of the kids had…on their phones…?"

I swallow back dry sand. "I tripped and fell and got my lunch all over myself. It was just embarrassing, that's all. My shirt's still soaking where it got stained."

What a happy memory lane to head down.

"Lila, she sent me the recordings."

I drop my gaze and squeeze my eyes tight shut. I'm going to cry. I'm going to cry. Fuzzwhat headbutts my hand, and I hang onto her for courage.

"Are you...have you been seeing things...like your mother?"

"No."

"I've seen the video—"

"They were there. They were right there. You just can't see them on the video, that's all. There is such a thing as creative editing. You can do anything you want these days online, and people just believe it." My tears are betraying me one stream at a time. "I'm the new girl. You know how it goes. Next week, it will be someone else's turn."

His fingers crush the empty can. You can almost feel him itching to get another one. He's silent. Silent as the grave. He's always been the type to think before he speaks. Doesn't rush in, boots and all. Gives thought a wide berth first.

I hate it. It's like opening up a big chasm for me to fall into.

"You know your mother..." His voice breaks, but then he finds the fire instead of the compassion. "I can't have it again, Lila. I can't. Now, are you telling me the truth? Or are you covering up what's really going on? Because I won't have liars in my house. Your guidance counsellor wants you to go for testing—"

"What?" My tears vanish. "What for?"

"She's concerned."

"There's nothing wrong."

"It's to check. These things can run in the family. Genetics. It's precautionary."

"But I'm fine."

"Then the tests will say that."

My breathing's so ragged I can't catch it. There's an intense pain in my throat that's shutting off my words, choking me. "But, but, but…"

"There's no 'buts' about it, Lila. I don't want what happened to your mother to happen to you. That's not the life I want for you."

"What about the life I want for me?"

"You're too young to make these decisions, and so long as you're under my roof, you'll obey my rules. Now, I'm sorry, but you'll be going for testing whether you like it or not."

His voice is raised, and it's sending my heart rate into overdrive. I want to punch him. Hard. In the mouth. Crack his lip.

"I will not. I will not end up like her." I'm sobbing and shouting and blubbering. "I'm not her."

"You don't understand."

"I do. I was *there*. She was my mother. I was *there*." And I didn't believe her too. Guilt's eating me up from the inside out. "Don't tell me who I am and who I'm not. That's nothing to do with you."

There's a cold fury in my father's expression. "You will get to your room. Now."

"I'm going."

Fuzz makes a strange eek sound as I snatch her back from my father's negative, ugly mood. Send me for tests? How dare he? He has no right. He's not the boss of me. He knows nothing about me. And as for eyelash lady, she can go suck it.

My schoolbag's still on my back. I stomp out the kitchen, wishing there was a door to slam. How can he do this to me?

Does he want me to end up in The Parks, just like Mom?

What does he think will happen when I fail those

tests?

That they'll say, "It's okay, she can carry on without meds and interventions and checking in for a 'rest'?"

Ha! Fat chance of that!

Listen, Mrs. Guidance Counsellor, firstly, no one wears those big falsies in the middle of the day anymore, and secondly, there's no point asking about my future if you're the one trying to take it away from me.

I do slam my bedroom door. It doesn't have enough force behind it, though. Should I do it a second time?

No. I don't want him coming up here.

He knows nothing about anything.

Nothing at all.

Chapter 29

Missing people

I wake early. Fuzzwhat's eye is worse than ever. Glued shut and weeping.

I don't know what to do.

Grace mentioned a vet close by. Maybe before school…that's ridiculous. School starts so early here.

An emergency vet will chew through the tiny savings I have from my online hauls. It has to be done, though.

I look up their location. Open. A little luck.

There's part of me that hopes that Dad was drunk enough to forget everything that happened last night. Not that he'd be that drunk—I don't wish for that. Just that he'd forget.

I don't want to think about it. First priority has to be Fuzz. "I promise I'll find you a good home, the best home. One where you get lots of treats, and lots of attention, the best sun spots, all the furniture you can claw, all the ornaments you can shove off a desk."

We've had a cat before. Bobby. My mom's cat. Followed her everywhere. Slept in a bed on her bed (cat and small-dog owners will get me). Also a black cat. He'd been found on the streets, and my mom had rescued him. He swaggered rather than walked and tarted himself round the neighborhood—outside cats are more a thing back home. Everyone loved Bobby.

The vet's room is on the back of a house that looks exactly like ours. One reception, three chairs, and a single consulting room. Only the vet's there, and she sees me right away, which is a handy thing because Fuzzwhat's loving being wrapped up like a burrito in my blanket. The walk here was perilous, to say the least.

The vet gives Fuzzwhat the once over, hands me some drops, and lets me know I have to sterilize her.

I know, I know.

"Is okay, Fuzz, you're in the best hands now," I reassure her as the vet hands her back to me.

I don't know who's more surprised when I head back out of the consulting room, Grace or me?

"Oh, you brought her here!" Grace is school-ready, her bag on her back. She bounds over to make a fuss of Fuzz, aahing and cooing.

I mean, I can't blame her.

"Hey, Mom, this is my friend from school, Lila."

Mom? The vet. The kind lady vet who can help out? Is her mom? Talk about small-town vibes.

"We've met." The vet says and turns her attention to Fuzz. "And I've now met Fuzzie too."

Grace picks up another bag from behind the reception counter. "You want to walk to school together?"

"I need to drop Fuzz off."

"We've got time. Bye, Mom, see you later!" Grace is already holding the door open for me.

The door clatters behind us.

"I'm glad you came to see her. She's the best."

There's a huge swell of pride in Grace's voice that would be flat-out missing if I had to speak about my dad right now.

"I knew she could help you. She didn't charge, right?"

"Nope…but I could pay," I hasten to add. In case she thinks I'm a mooch.

"I said you'd be bringing her in, so to keep an eye out."

She's so matter-of-fact I'm guessing her mom is the only vet in town.

"That's very kind of you. Thank you."

We walk in silence for a few steps or so.

Fuzz is wriggling something shocking. What I need is a cat carrier. Nope, what I need is a miracle because I don't want to lose Fuzz, but I can't keep her either.

"I'm sorry about what happened. You know. At the cafeteria." She pauses and concentrates on her fingers, which she's interlacing in a series of patterns. "You know, we had this one kid a few years ago—he joined us from some big city, I forget which. I mean, when you're a kid, you don't remember details, right?" She takes her phone out her pocket, opens the screen, scrolls, then closes it again, back in the pocket. "Anyhoo, so he was hella clumsy. My grandfather would say he was a "klutz" since he used to trip over his own feet. And he always wore this baseball cap, like everywhere, that had dinosaurs on it, you know, from the movie. This cap used to get carried away by the wind, fall for daaayyyysss, you know?"

"Yeah, I get it. Clumsy."

Grace is watching now for my reaction like there's some sort of test I need to pass. She does the finger thing again. "What do you know about Pinedale High?"

"That there's a block system, and don't eat the

chicken thingies."

She whoops. "Totally agreed. All the sauce in the world can't hide how dodgy those things are."

"Yeah, Joe warned me, but I forgot."

"True story. But seriously, you haven't heard the stories…Didn't you say your dad went here?"

"Yep, back in the nineties."

"And he said nothing?"

We reach my house. "He might say something now if he sees me out here with Fuzz. Give me a sec."

I creep like a ninja back into the house, up the stairs, and into my room. After showering her with a thousand non-consensual kisses, I fill up her treats and close the door tight. Please let her be here when I get home.

My father's at the foot of the stairs. Did he see me? Dang. He did. "Morning."

A grunt is what I want to give him. "Hi. Need to get to school."

"We're not done talking about this," he reminds me.

"I'm done," I mumble.

"Did you say something?" Mean Dad Mode is in full flight.

"Have a good day." My tone suggests the opposite.

I scamper out of there. I totally forgot Grace was waiting for me.

She's rehearsing with air pom-poms. "Everything okay?"

"Never better. How's your grandfather?"

"Much the same. Mom says he's starting to drift between this world and the next. Apparently, that's what happens when it's time. The veil drops. He's talking a lot about things that happened years ago. He gets confused. Mixes us up with someone else."

"Sorry to hear that. It's rough. Same thing happened with my mom. For different reasons, though."

We don't say much of anything else for the rest of the walk. Grace practices her cheers, and I cheer her and her superior co-ordination.

It's a welcome distraction from ghosts and cats that need to go into welfare and horrible fathers who want to have their daughters committed for being bullied in a cafeteria.

And no, I know I can't say that. Not out loud.

When we arrive at Pinedale High, the teachers are gathering up students to the main hall.

"Something's up," says Grace, and we slide into the stream.

"Is it an assembly?"

"The principal probably wants to talk to us."

"Are we in trouble?"

Grace surveys the situation. "It's definitely serious."

We find a seat and wait as the hall fills up.

Whispers buzz.

Principal Kouriki's behind a lectern, stern and stoic.

She reminds me of those old Viking women, ready for battle.

A second later, a police officer joins her on stage.

It's dead quiet now.

"Students, we're joined by Officer Tod Michaels today. One of our students, Joseph Stoneburgh, has gone missing."

A deathly silence.

My heart sinks to the bottom of my stomach. Missing? The *dream*. That means he's…I don't want to think about it.

Officer Michaels looks around the room. "If anyone

has any information as to Joseph's whereabouts…"
   I want to throw up.
   Who would believe me?
   What would I *say?*

Chapter 30

When you know, you know

"If anyone has any information about the whereabouts of your school friend, be sure to let us know. You can visit the principal, and we'll take it from there." Officer Michaels sits.

Joe. Missing.

I want to put my hand up.

Yeah, and say what? That he's in an underground cave somewhere near a rock pool on the south side of the woods? Because that wouldn't sound suspicious at all, nuh-uh.

There would be questions.

How do I know?

Was I with him?

Did he say something?

It's been a few days since that dream. I can almost taste the dehydration. And his leg! I'd almost forgotten that.

Wait! If I dreamed about him at all, then he's...he's already gone. I'm conversing with ghost Joe.

It's a peculiar feeling. My legs want to hustle me straight into the woods to go search for the area I can picture perfectly. But my anxiety is putting out a giant *Whooooaaaaa, where do you think you're going?* And right at the bottom is this terrible giant sadness. All of

Joe's beautiful dreams about his future are languishing in the bottom of that cave. He'll never be an environmental scientist, or save the world with his eco-warrior ways, or open up an eco-village for tourists who want to experience the great outdoors. It's all gone.

It's a horrible sadness. All that unlived life, and for what?

"You okay?" Grace side-eyes me, then whispers. "You seem twitchy."

"I'm thinking of the woods."

"Joe knows those woods inside and out."

A kid turns round to shush us.

Gee, thanks.

He *knew* those woods inside and out, and look where it got him. Dying alone in a cave. I've got to tell someone. No, I need to head out there, try to find where he is. Joe is not going to be another student who disappears in the woods. That doesn't feel fitting for someone who motivated so many, was a captain of the football, and the champion of punctuality.

My heart sinks again. Grace will be devastated.

I shuffle about my seat. The principal talks and I hear none of her words. My mind's scenario planning this afternoon.

Which way is south?

How to rock climb?

Can my phone get a signal out there?

"And students, before you think of launching your own search party, the woods will be out of bounds for the next few days until the police have concluded their own investigations. You are welcome to join the official search party, which will meet at the entrance to the woods at four this evening. Please bring a flashlight."

Why are they looking in the dark?

They'll never find him.

Look at me, speaking as if he hasn't already...*succumbed* to his injuries. I can't bring myself to say "dead," not just yet.

My insides swim round my belly. What if I run into his ghost? Will he know he's a ghost? Or will he be asking me for soil samples for the rest of my time in this school?

What if he *doesn't* turn into a ghost?

My brain can't handle all the possible permutations of this.

I sink my head in my hands.

Principal Kouriki leads the procession past the students. The atmosphere is grimmer than the worst English winter. It's grey, chilly and thick with dread. Not even a phone pings.

If anyone has any information...

I have to join the search party. Conveniently become separated and find those rocks. Surely finding a big 'ole clump of rocks can't be that difficult?

We amble toward class. Grace loops her arm in mine, and it reminds me of being with Jo when things were so much simpler. No ghosts, no dead mothers, no dead buddies. Only living things, like hopes, dreams, and chats about which of the boy-band members were a total snack.

"He probably went to the south side of the woods. He likes to head there when things get...heated. You know. At home?" Grace's voice crackles with worry. "If he's lost in those woods, he'll be able to get back."

"Three days, though?"

"Yeah. I hear you."

I'm soft-pedaling the inevitable. I can't blurt out, "Sorry, Grace, he's gone." She'll think I'm mad. But I can't really prepare her for the worst either. That seems even more awful. Like holding a damaging secret that eats away at everyone who holds it, even if it's for a second.

"I don't feel like he's passed away, though," she says. "But he's definitely in trouble." There's great certainty in her voice, which makes this a thousand times worse. "I feel it. You know? When you get that gut feeling?"

"Sure." What if I can't get away from the search party? What if they post policemen to patrol the red tape there? And I can't get past them?

Agh! There's no one I can tell. What if I get lost in the same place?

Officer Michaels and his mates loiter.

I should be able to go up to them and tell them what I know. Yes, I'll do it.

Now.

My heart rate speeds up like I'm about to shoot down the highest slide at the water park. It's that same adrenaline-spiked thum thum thump. He's getting closer closer closer. Now.

I'll do it *now*.

I take a deep breath and keep walking. Straight past. I can't do this. He'll tell the guidance counsellor, and she'll tell my father. Or they'll both tell my father, and then I'll be sent away to The Parks to sit with people who drool and wear adult diapers and who think they're President Reagan.

I'm going to have to head into those woods.

"...because I often get those convictions, and

they're never wrong. Haven't been wrong yet."

My ears tune back to Grace. I've missed every word.

"When we were kids, he and I would go adventuring in the woods," she says. "There's this one part he really likes, but it's off track. I wonder if he went there?"

My brain processes this new information—I can almost hear the cogs click. "You know your way around the woods?"

She nods. "I feel like...I think he's there. That's what my gut's telling me."

"Perhaps we should...go...look." He'll be gone when we get there, but we can make sure his family knows. His brothers.

"You mean with the search party?"

My voice thickens. "Ye-es." There's no plan forming, more of a "happy accident" of Grace's true confessions and my need for a woods guide. The rest I can blur through. Pinedale Swish through. Joe had mentioned the south side when he talked about getting more soil samples. That could be a place to start. A white lie meets a truth meets necessity. We could head out with the search party and then get lost ourselves. If Grace knows where we are...

It's plausible, any other day of the week, no one would think twice. Heck, Joe and I shimmied into the woods together the other day, and everything was a-okay.

Grace considers this. "We should. That's the best way to go about this. We can't go wandering off ourselves."

"No, no, I'd never suggest that." Wouldn't I?

I know where he is. I simply need to find him.

"So, we're doing this?"

"Yes."

Isn't that how all bad ideas start?

Chapter 31

Best laid plans

Four o'clock looms.

I ran, okay, speed walked back home, gave Fuzzwhat her drops, and left a note for my dad. Will he read it? It's on the next six-pack of beer in the fridge. There's not a wedge of cheese, but there's beer for daaaaayyys. Priorities.

He might read it.

Experience has taught me that he'll avoid me for a few days before ambushing me with that psychiatric test. He'll simply scoop me out of school and drive me there. I won't get a further say in it.

I cannot wait to have my own home. Or rental. The reality is that I might not own anything in this lifetime. A space that's all my own. With as many cats as I want.

I'm in my trainers. *Sneakers*. Are they designed for trekking in the woods? No. Neither are my track pants or my hoodie. They'll have to do. I've also packed some water, snacks, a torch, tissues, and a box of matches.

And, oh boy, have I misinterpreted this situation or what?

Ready to search for Joe, there are parents, police, students, a few pet dogs, a very angry-looking man with a backward baseball cap who's pacing up and down with a phone in his hand, and the principal dressed in activewear and a giant puffer jacket. Which looks strange. Like seeing her doing her grocery shopping or waiting in the doctor's office.

Officer Michaels brandishes a bullhorn that he's using any excuse to press into action. "The search will be underway at exactly oh sixteen hundred hours. Make sure to follow the officers leading the various parties. Make sure you know who your team are."

Doubt is eating up any confidence I have. How are we supposed to sneak off if we're being checked in?

Grace hovers on the outskirts of the woods' entrance.

I hurry up to her. "There are so many people here."

She brings me up to speed. "They're splitting us up, north, south, east, west. We need to follow Officer Michaels—he's the south-side leader."

My insides pale at that. There was an orderly at The Parks who reminds me of Officer Michaels. Same big build and a no-nonsense approach that's also hard as steel underneath. Their way or no way. And they're happy to use brute force to get it. Don't get me wrong, I never saw anyone harmed at The Parks. But they had these sticks…batons…that they kept on their waistband. In case there was trouble.

Officer Michaels has that same look. Like he'd like trouble to call because then he could use his baton, and no one would ask any questions.

We shuffle to the south side pack, careful to keep to the fringes. A register is being sent round. Grace raises her eyebrows.

"They're too busy looking for Joe to notice," I reassure her, scribbling my name in my worst handwriting possible. Joined up style. Old-fashioned scrawl.

"We don't do that here," says Grace, tidily printing out her details. Does she want to get caught?

A tall, thin man who could disappear behind a lamppost brushes past us. He's not wearing a jacket. He looks like he's arrived straight from some office job in a fancy shirt and tie. Proper shoes too. Int-er-es-ting.

Grace whispers. "Sometimes you can tell when someone doesn't belong."

Harsh. But true. "He's here to help, though."

"A teacher, I think."

Ah, that's why he looks familiar. Something about the distinct shape of his face, the way his chin points. I've definitely seen that face around here.

He cuts through the crowds with ease, finding his way to near where Officer Michaels is repeating the time over the bullhorn.

I mean, in this day and age, everyone has a phone or a tracker or something that tells the time. He obvs likes the sound of his own voice.

Finally, the search is underway.

Not going to lie – it's an adrenaline buzz. All these bodies pushing through the forest, searching and calling.

Like we're tracking him.

Sam's dream comes back to haunt me. They were tracking *them*. And it was terrifying.

Pretty soon, the group spreads out. And every now and then someone calls out, "Joe!"

Officer Michaels has one hand on his gun as he struts.

The teacher is a few feet ahead of him. That's a surprise. I can't imagine Officer Michaels as the type to share the glory. Maybe I'm wrong?

A few minutes later, I get my bearings. "This is where Joe and I found our soil from. There! There's the log I sat on." I rush forward. "Yep, this is where that old anthill is. I recognize it. He said he'd come back here." I point in the direction he did. "And look for better soil."

Grace nods. "Makes sense. This is one of his favorite parts. We used to hang out close to here."

"So you've known him forever?"

"Sure. He used to live next door with his brothers. We spent most of elementary school together. His mom would leave the boys at my house in the afternoon. Then he moved to one of those big houses out on Oak Avenue. He stayed the same, though. Same ole Joe."

There's a regret in her voice. "It's not the same though. It gets different when you get older. Things aren't as easy."

"I get it. The one thing I want is for things to stay the same. And life has other plans."

"Sucks."

"Sucks balls."

"Damn right." Grace switches to all work, no fun. "So, between those two trees is a trail. It's not used anymore. They closed it up years ago. Joe would explore beyond there all the time."

I make sure none of the rest of the party is anywhere within earshot. "You think that's where he is?"

"If he's in these woods, he's out there."

"He's in here all right."

Grace nods. "I believe you."

Well, that makes a change.

"Officer Michaels," I yell.

He whips his head in my direction, alert, attentive.

"What about the trail down there?" I indicate the two

trees.

"That's been off-limits for decades now."

"Yes, but what if he went down there?"

"It's off-limits."

"Yeah, but who would stop him?" This seemed a reasonable response. Negative.

"Young lady, you would be careful to remember who you are talking to, ain't that right?"

"Yes."

His nose is straight, and his eyebrows bushy. "Yes?"

"Yes, sir?"

"That's better." He brushes imaginary dirt from his shirtsleeves.

Oh, I called this one right. He is like that orderly. A great, big, ugly jerk. And a bully.

He spits something thick and dark out of his mouth. "Now, that part of the woods is inaccessible. That means neither he nor anyone else would be down there. Like I said, it's off-limits." There's complete conviction in his tone.

Him? Wrong? Am I mad? Who am I to suggest such a thing? "But what if he is…Sir?

"Are you telling me I'm wrong?"

Yes. You are 100% wrong. I don't answer him.

The teacher's looking back at me with a suitably stern expression.

"No, sir, but—"

"I'm leading this team through these woods in a search for your friend. I would appreciate it if you let me do my job." He purposefully marches away from the trail.

I'm boiling with anger. I didn't even have to mention dreams or ghosts or supernatural anything, and he didn't want to listen to me. Being a kid sucks. Sucks big hairy balls big time.

Nothing like being proven right.

Grace huddles close. "So, we're not heading into the trail?"

"We're so heading into the trail."

Chapter 32

Seeing things

This might not be the best idea I've ever had.

I don't do green, and I'm surrounded by walls of it.

Grace bunny hops through the woods like she's at one with everything living.

Ha ha! Some gallows humor. I'm at one with everything dead.

Any second now, we'll make a turn or fight our way through a mass of vegetation, and there will be the rocky outcrop or the pool or even the mouth of the cave, and I will be vindicated.

To myself.

I *am* having vivid dreams of ghosts' deaths.

This is not a drill.

And it has nothing to do with mental illness and everything to do with genetics. I bet my grandmother or one of her three sisters had weird dreams too.

Then, I can figure out a way to stop them.

The gentle hum of the forest seems to be getting louder.

"Do you hear that? That revving sound?"

Grace is a good few steps ahead of me. She tilts her head. "The crickets?"

"No, the…wood chipper? That buzzing? It's getting closer."

"Nope."

It's probably some giant man-eating snake rattling about under these leaves. I pick up my pace.

The trail suddenly drops down into what can only be described as a ravine. "Now, that was unexpected." Any wrong move and you'll slide straight down into the rocks below.

Grace picks her footing with care. "I think this is why they closed off this part. Make sure your feet are parallel with the slope."

I copy Grace's movements and feel less like I'm moments from plunging. "I need a big walking stick to balance."

"You're doing great. Don't turn your feet forward. Yeah, like that."

"I can see why Officer Michaels didn't want the search party trekking down here. You don't want a search party for the search party."

"My grandfather researched Pinedale High's history as part of some genealogical society thing."

"Genie…A say what now?"

"Family histories, family trees, that kind of thing. He's a local authority round here. Well, he was. Now he gives me the score to football matches we watched together. Short-term memory's fried. Anyhoo, he said that the reason it was closed off was because a student had become injured out here and—"

"They never found the body."

"They did but too late. He'd already passed away. They found his bike down there." She points to a particularly lethal collection of pointy rocks. "He hit his head. Must've hauled ass down here and been unable to stop."

Sam. Sam died down here.

My steps slow down. Oh, Sam, what a horribly lonely and scary way to go. I want to rush back to the senior girls' bathroom and hug them until their pain fades away.

Grace rests her balance on a larger boulder. "I don't know why he came riding through here in the first place. None of it's bike-friendly."

"They were chased. And it was dark. They didn't have a choice." Conflicting emotions vie for my attention. Justice for Sam has overridden any common sense, which, contrary to popular belief, is not all that common either. "Or that's what might have happened. Just saying."

We tiptoe through the rock field. Sam would only ever be out here if they were chased. This is no more their natural habitat than mine. What were the reports that went out? An accident? Teenager decides to go for a late-night bike ride through the woods? My heart's aching for them.

They deserved so much more.

There's no sign marked *X, here's the spot*. No twisted bike metal. No sign of a memorial or a plaque. Only leaves.

The bracelet!

What am I thinking?

Sam died over thirty years ago.

There's no pink ribbon waiting for me to pick up and return to its owner.

Does it stop me from looking? What do you think? I scan every available surface, but short of getting on my hands and knees and scouring every inch of the area, I'm not stumbling over anything, pink or not.

"You know, my grandfather has plenty of the history on this place. He might even have some reports from the accident." Grace drops the offer in all casual-like. "You can always ask him, you know. To find out what happened."

I know what happened, I yell in my head. They're in the bathroom, you ask them yourself. They'll tell you themself.

Get yourself together, Lila. This is not Grace's fault. "Yeah, I'll do that. Sounds interesting."

"It is. And he loves to talk about it. He'll tell you all about the things that have been happening at the school pretty much since Day One. The good and the bad. He doesn't sugarcoat things. He's the first to say how it's haunted and who by. Like that bathroom you were in. There are stories that there's a girl who haunts it. A giantess. If you look into the mirror, you can see her looking back at you."

This shaves right up against my bones. Sam's always busy at the mirror. But I can see them standing in front of me too. "Have you seen them?"

"None of them. And believe me, I've been searching. All of the most haunted. The old hall is obvs one of the big ones, with the fire."

"Obvs."

"But I haven't seen one yet. I've even been on the school grounds for camps and nothing. The whole night searching for a supernatural phenomenon. Not even a cold chill."

"That sounds... disappointing." Imagine wishing ghosts on yourself. Why would anyone do that?

"It's the worst." Grace dashes her fists against her thighs in frustration.

Hey, I'd happily do a swap.

"Riley, who sits two over from you in English, he swears there's a gang of poltergeists. Sometimes, books will toss themselves across the classroom. Or they'll throw chalk or markers. It's wild."

"Yeah. I take your word for it. Seriously, though, what's with that buzzing noise? I swear it's getting louder." It is. And it's following us.

Grace contemplates. "Maybe they've got a drone?"

"That checks out." Ish. The canopy above us is very picky about letting any light in, let alone a drone. But yes, why not use a drone to scan the area?

We push forward and swiftly reach a space that splits into two arms. Left or right?

"I'm not sure which is the way he'd go," admits Grace.

I'm half-listening because that buzzing sound? It's more like three buzzing sounds, each one overlapping the next. Three drones?

"This arm takes us round the back of the woods, I'm pretty certain. But the left arm...I don't know." Grace surveys our situation—fading light, difficult choice, no map.

"You really don't hear that?" It's worryingly close, whatever it is.

We both look up.

Only it's not coming from above us. It's behind us. Motorbikes. Ghostly motorbikes? Is that a thing? It must be. Because I recognize the drivers.

The Bruno brothers.

Chapter 33

The dead honest truth

They're closing in fast.

One by one, the gang surrounds me. Well, us. But Grace can't see them. Oh My God. She can't see them. "Here are the ghosts you ordered," I mumble.

It's the cafeteria all over again.

Eugene cuts the bike's engine. How does that work? A ghost bike? Are they imagining it? Is it real? "Told you to keep to your own kind. But you wouldn't listen."

"Lila, we have to step it up." Grace sounds like she's in another dimension. The real one. With human, tangible things. Not ghostly spirits.

Eugene blocks my way. "Where do you think you're going?"

Don't speak. Don't speak. Don't speak.

Evan sits astride on his phantom bike, his arms resting on the handlebars. He can't meet my gaze.

Charlie joins his brother. "What's the matter? Cat got your tongue?"

That expression's always baffled me. Which cat? And why? Cats catch mice or birds or bats, not tongues.

"Looks like she's ignoring us, boys. There's a penalty for that." He winds up his arm as if he were swinging a bat.

"Lila, what's up? You look scared." Ah, and now

Grace has gone and blown it. What did you tell them that for?

I can't see beyond the brothers' shoulders, but I can hear her feet crunching through the forest.

"Do you think Officer Michaels is coming back this way?"

Eugene snorts at Grace's suggestion. "Officer Michaels? Come to fetch? Rescue you from the big bad wolf in the woods. Hey, little girl, don't cha know he can't see her? She's not here, Red."

Charlie's making faces at Grace, pulling raspberries, crossing his eyes, making lewd gestures.

Have to give it to Grace, she was dead right—she can't see ghosts for shit. She walks straight past the brothers. Not through them, though. "Does it feel colder here, Grace?"

"No, should it?" Her brow creases.

"I don't know which of you is dumber?" Eugene's hitting his stride. "The one who's acting like we're not here, or the one who pretends she's still one of them."

"Lila? You have such a weird look on your face. Did you see something?" Grace waits patiently for me to respond.

"I have nothing." This is the truth. I have no idea how to handle the three ghosts in our company who are threatening us with...*something* and who are now speaking in riddles, which, to be fair, I thought was beyond their mental capacities.

Boom! The wind is pushed from my chest, and I'm hurtling backward. One moment, I'm standing, the next, I'm on my butt. It takes a second to find my breath.

Eugene spits to the side, reminding me of Officer Michaels. "No more talking. You need to be taught a lesson. And lookie here, you've got a willing teacher."

"What happened?" Grace is by my side, confused. "You just...*pow!*" Her fingers gather up the air. "How did you do that? You went...*backward*?"

She looks around for the answer. Who ironically is standing right next to her.

I brush the dirt from my hands. "And you're not feeling a chill in the air?" I give each word a pointed menace. C'mon, Grace, what were we talking about earlier? Don't make me say it out loud.

Where's telepathy when you need it?

Two seconds later, I'm back on my butt.

"C'mon, guys, leave them alone." It's Evan. "It's enough already."

"What's going on?" Grace reaches out to me. Right behind her, Charlie's coming in with both palms up, ready to push. The look on his face is pure delight. Creep.

"Watch out!"

Too late! Grace lands on top of me.

Immediately, she picks herself up and pushes back on her hands, scrabbling to the nearest tree. "What the hell is going on? What was that? Lila, what's happening?"

Eugene high-fives Charlie.

Yeah. Way to go, loser.

"I said, leave them alone," repeats Evan. "They're not bothering anybody."

"Hey, what's with you? You going chicken on us?" Charlie squawks and pecks his head, his arms bent and flapping at the waist. "Chicken, chicken, chickaw."

I go out of orbit. "You're nothing but sad-ass bullies. Can't you think of something better to do with all your time? All of eternity, and you're carrying on like mean little boys."

"Mean little boys," mocks Eugene.

"Lila? What? Who are you talking to?"

Grace is so pale that if you told me there was a vampire nearby, I'd believe you.

"The Bruno brothers, Charlie and Eugene, and Evan. Ghosts. They're ghosts." Right, it's out now.

"We're ghosts. Did you hear that, boys? Ghosts. Oooooohhhhhh."

Charlie chases after his brother in an impression of some man-in-a-sheet ghost movie. Or that cartoon with the orange dog. I forget the name.

"Boo!"

"Ghosts?" Grace's lip's trembling. Her eyes are wider than a Pekinese. Then she smiles. "There are ghosts? Here? Now? And you can feel them?"

"See them."

"Like in the cafeteria? There were ghosts? You were shouting at ghosts?"

"The very same ghosts."

Charlie resumes his leader-of-the-pack stance. "Hey, *you*—the dead don't answer to the living."

Is he pointing at me? "How am I dead?"

Evan jumps in. "I tried to say—"

"You're not dead?" Eugene enters the fray. "How come you're talking to us?"

"Are they speaking to you now? What are they saying? Do they have a message from the other side?" Grace looks everywhere but at the three of them.

It's disconcerting.

"Can you hear them?"

"Sadly, very well."

"How are you not dead?" Charlie can't seem to

grasp reality. "I don't understand. This one's a transfer from Halford."

Halford? "What's that?"

Grace shouts. "What do you want to know?"

We all look at her in some dismay. It's true.

Then it dawns on me—this is what I look like to everyone else. *Mental.* "What's Halford?" I ask her.

"Town cemetery. Wait, what's happening? Do they want to go there?"

"You thought I was in from *the cemetery*?" I can't keep the temerity from my voice. The *cemetery*?

"I told you she was living. But no, you had to go and get involved." Evan sounds like a tired parent. "Dumbass."

"Hey! Who you callin' a dumbass!" Eugene's fists are out, ready to deliver. "You want a knuckle sandwich?"

"They don't like sharing the school with the living. It's their thing," explains Evan. "Why you out here in the woods? That dude who dresses like a chick died out here, ya know? Ya gotta be careful." He's chewing at the skin around his thumb.

"What are they saying, Lila? Don't keep me in the dark." Grace can barely contain her excitement.

Where do I start to explain this drama? "We're out here to find our friend, Joe. He went missing."

"Lots of kids go missing out here," says Evan. "There's one they didn't find out in the cave."

"The cave?" The dream. "Where's that?"

Grace corrects me. "There's no cave, Lila, that's a myth. If it was here, my grandfather would know."

"Ain't no myth, lady," says Eugene. "You're standing on it."

Chapter 34

Going underground

"I ain't no guide," says Charlie. He gives a
dismissive wave. "I'm not helping no one out. Especially
one of your kind."

Such a gallant, charming individual.

"You split, I'll show them the way," says Evan.

Eugene and Charlie sulk into the woods. One
moment, they're there, the next, gone. Motorbikes too.

So many questions.

"Lila, what is going on?" Grace smacks her hands
on her thighs in frustration. "Do they know where Joe
is?"

"Quick update. There were three, now there's one.
Evan. He's blond, in case you need a picture. About the
same height as Joe, thinner, though. He's standing to
your right."

Grace's head snaps to the right. She looks straight
past him.

Sigh. "He'll lead the way to the cave entrance. And
yes, there's a cave, and it extends underneath the
woods."

"This is so exciting," says Grace. "You can see them
and talk to them. Amazing."

Amazing, Grace. Ha! Should be a song. "Well, were
it not for them kicking our collective butt, you would not

believe me."

"Actually, you should thank my grandfather. He's obsessed with the Pinedale High hauntings. I was trying to tell you about that new guy. I always thought he could see them."

"Are we gonna stand here gabbing or get going?" Evan adjusts his jacket, pulling up the collar. "Last time I checked, humans can't see too well in the dark."

"I've got my torch." I pat my bag. "We'll follow you."

"Let's get cracking then." Evan moves through the woods like you or I would, but there's no sound. When he sets foot on leaves, no crunch, no scrunch, no nothing. "Your friend might have fallen through one of the cracks. That's what happened to the other guy."

"How do you know all this?" I need to piece together how their world works.

"We stick together, you know? Show each other the ropes. Watch out for that poison ivy, right there." Evan walks straight through it.

"Watch out, poison ivy," I say to Grace, who trots behind me. "Oh, and the ground's unstable in patches."

"There are cracks," corrects Evan.

"There are cracks."

"Ask him why he's here," says Grace.

"I can hear her, you know," confirms Evan. "Beats me."

"He doesn't know." It's getting colder. I pull my jacket tighter round me. There's a series of bigger rocks ahead. Boulders. "Don't tell me we have to climb over those?"

"I won't, then," says Evan. Wise guy. He has no problem scaling the rocks. "Use your legs to push up rather than your arms to pull up. Got it?"

Grace scales the challenge like some sort of gazelle. "Which way is he going?"

I lumber behind her. "That way."

Contrary to Evan's advice, Grace has to pull my ass over most of the rocks. "Clearly, you two were rock climbers in another life. No offense, Evan."

He's not listening to me. He's already charging ahead, scoping out the view from some ledge. The sun's dipping fast and furious.

Who starts a search party in the late afternoon? Early morning. That's when you head out.

"Ah, cool, Lila. A rock pool. Look!" Grace points at the shimmering water below.

"Here! This is where he was." The rocks, the pools… "He fell in somewhere around here."

"Fell in?" Grace's voice cracks. "What do you mean? How do you know?"

"I had a dream, that's all."

"When? Why didn't you say anything?"

"Because it was a dream. Last night, I dreamed that I was back in nursery school. Eating kiddie clay and worrying about algebra."

She pauses. "I take your point."

"Cave entrance's up there." Evan rubs imaginary dirt from his hands. "You're gonna need a flashlight."

"Yes, I have my torch."

"Torch?" He raises an eyebrow.

"Or we could make one of those torches from a branch and light them?" I've watched too many adventure movies.

"No fire," says Evan in almost a whisper.

"We can use my flashlight." Grace lights up the

woods like a stadium. She is master and commander of the flashlight, yielding it like a dangerous weapon. "I'll check for the cracks." The spotlight swings from left to right as Grace sweeps over the terrain.

Evan clears his throat. "I've been hoping you'd help me out."

I remember his freaking me out in the cafeteria, his perpetual loitering, the photo! "I'm listening."

"Music to my ears. I told the boys you were real. They didn't want to believe me. Their loss. It's easy to forget who you were when you're here, on our side. It's difficult to hold onto. You have to remember and be who you were, or you get lost. Time don't work the same here."

His voice thickens. "So, I had this brother, Beau. I can remember his name, that he loved baseball, his dog, Butch, and scaling smokes from my Ma. That's it. No, no, that's not it. I did it, you see. I brought him with us. Ma had me watch him. We had a fight, the boys and I. We didn't see eye to eye on this prank, and then the hall went, whoosh, up in flames. I went back to get him, I did. I couldn't, I didn't, I wasn't sure…"

He takes out a cigarette, lights it. There's no smoke.

"You do me a favor? Find him for me? Did he get out?" He runs his hand through his hair. His face is taut with guilt. "I wouldn't ask ordinarily…I don't want to disturb the living…you all get here soon enough, but…I gotta know."

"Beau?"

"Yeah. I've lost our family name. It's gone. Only thing that keeps you here is the feelings, you know?"

I could only guess. "I'll try to find him."

"He's twelve. A real squirt."

He wouldn't be twelve now, that's for sure.

"Hey, guys, I think I've found something." Grace's shout would raise the dead. "Oh my God, Lila, it's…I think it's him."

I turn to Evan, but he's no longer there. Pulled the ole disappearing-into-the-ether trick.

My torch is no comparison to Grace's, but it's getting the job done. I hurry to where she's standing on a rocky outcrop, her mega light facing into the cracks.

"Look, Lila, there."

"What am I looking at?" There are shadows, more shadows and then… "Is that a trainer?"

"What? It's Joe's sneaker, I'm sure of it. Look at the laces. He always wears purple laces, Pinedale's colors."

I cannot say I had noticed this detail. "How do we get down there?"

"What does your ghost friend say?"

"Oh, he's gone."

"Gone? Where?"

"Ghost convention? Do you have any rope, I could lower you down?"

"Joe, Joe!" Grace calls.

My throat is in my mouth. What if we're too late? What if Joe's already been greeted by the Bruno brothers' ghostly welcoming committee? And is now haunting the biology lab for all eternity? Or worse. What if he's not a ghost? He's just *gone*?

"Maybe I can—"

"Grace, is that you?"

It's faint and it's weak, but it's Joe.

189

Chapter 35

He's alive!

"You're still here!" It's the wrong thing to say.
Grace grimaces. "*Still* here?"
"I thought...it doesn't matter. Don't worry, Joe,
we'll get you out."
There's a grunt.
We're now firmly in the dark.
"I can get down there," says Grace, shining her
flashlight into the crevice.
"Evan was on the money. One step to the side, and
you'd miss it, but if you're unlucky, straight down.
Cracks, indeed."
"You were on the money. You said he was out
here."
"Just a dream." An uncomfortable thought shouts
for my attention. What if you're a little bit psychic, too?
Please. No. I shove that line of thinking far, far, far away.
That's the last thing I need. Speaking to ghosts is one
thing. Having visions of the future, another. Maybe I
dreamed about Joe because he's reaching out and
touching death's hand?
"How long have you been down there?" My voice
echoes about the cave. A whole underground cave.
"Mom?" comes the reply.
"He's hallucinating," says Grace. "We have to get

him out of there."

"With what? I don't have any rope, you don't have any rope, and besides, there's nothing to tie it onto."

"I can definitely climb down there."

"And if you slip and fall? I definitely *can't* climb down there." Wrong shoes, for starters. "You saw me on those rocks."

"We have to do something." Grace is pulsing with nervous energy. She keeps clenching and unclenching her hands.

"Let's call for help." I dig my phone out of my pocket and look for the reception bars. One tiny block.

"Officer Michaels?"

"I don't have his number, do you?"

Grace shakes her head. "And my phone's dead."

My heart's somewhere in the pit of my stomach. There's no other answer.

—*Hey Dad, pls*—

Nope, that won't do. Delete.

—*Hi Dad, we're stuck here. Pls hlp.* ☺—

I drop a pin. And send.

One tick.

I swing the phone into the air. "No reception."

"Watch your step," warns Grace.

Bit late now. Dad will go off the deep end at this one. If he gets the message, if he reads the message, and if he controls his temper for long enough to alert the authorities.

I. Am. So. Dead.

—*We found our friend who was lost in the woods.*—

—*Got lost from search party.*—

—*Xx*—

Send. One tick.

—And pls brng ambulance. Friend in cave.—

"Don't worry, Joe, you're gonna be okay." Grace has a tremor in her voice which indicates she is far from okay. "We've called Lila's dad for help."

"Maybe we should call 999 as well."

"911."

"Right." I punch in the digits. "…no signal."

"What should we do now?"

"Wait?"

There's no moon. It's dark, can't-see-your-hand-in-front-of-you dark.

Grace hooks onto my arm. "They'll find us."

"Hopefully before the bears do."

"We wouldn't have found Joe if it wasn't for you, you know?"

"Someone might have stumbled on him." Literally.

"But you knew. And you spoke to *them*. The ghosts."

"Grace…please can we not mention that? The ghosts thing?"

"It's so cool, though."

Maybe it's the dark. I can't see Grace anymore; I can only feel her arm in mine. A safety. If I can't see you, you can't see me, vibe. "My mom used to be able to see ghosts too. You know what happened to her? She ended up in a sanatorium. They said that she was a paranoid schizophrenic and gave her drugs and all sorts of brain things. It was okay when it was only her and me and my dad. We knew about her 'gift.' Though it mostly looked like she was losing her mind. But it was one of her quirks. Like giving her cat, Bobby, an accent when she talked to him."

The guilt might shift one day, but right now, it

overwhelms me like thick, sticky tar, burnt black.

I continue my confession because I have to. I've kept it to me for all this time, and it stings. I have to tell the truth. My truth. To me.

"There was this fancy specialist who told her she'd help. That she believed her when she said she was in contact with the spirits. It was a lie, though. By then it was too late. The doctor boarded her up in this fancy place called The Parks, but it was a prison. They wanted to run experiments. They wanted to know what was on the other side, and they wanted to use my mother to give them their answers. We didn't know. Dad and I. The specialist said she didn't want to see us, that we didn't believe her tales. That we thought she was mad. It wasn't true, though. A month later, she unalived herself."

To say it out loud is to relive it all over again. The call. The realizations. The horror of it all. Grace's arm tightens on mine.

My face is wet with tears. "The last thing my dad needs to know is that I found Joe through the same 'gifts'."

Grace gives me a bear hug. "I got you."

The roar in my head lessens. Even if it's for a few minutes.

"The worst part is, she thinks I didn't believe her. That it was all her imagination. The last time I saw her, she told me the story about when she saw her first ghost. I'd heard it so many times before, I only half-paid attention. I realize now it was a warning. That the same thing might happen to me. And there would be nothing I could do to stop it."

"That sounds really tough."

"It was. It is."

There's a comfortable silence. It's the first time I can be myself since I got here. Well, this me, the new me who has a hotline to the other side.

Grace gives me space.

Then she changes the subject, for which I am eternally grateful.

"You found Joe, though. He and I...it's complicated."

He-he. I can't help but laugh. Seriously? "Weren't you the one who said 'it's complicated' means you don't want to deal?"

"Why would I incriminate myself like that? I plead the fifth."

"Okay, so what does that mean? I keep hearing it?"

"The fifth? 'You have the right to remain silent, you have the right to an attorney'…"

"Ah! Mystery solved."

"Joe's always looked out for me. He's like a best pal."

I can't see Grace's face, but I'm sure her cheeks are bright red.

"But?"

"No buts."

"So you don't like him, *like him*?"

"No, no, it's not like that." She's all flustered at that.

I bet she's trying to figure out what to do with her hands. "And yet, here you are. Following ghosts. In the woods. Close to midnight. Spill the tea, woman!"

"Lila, he can probably hear every word."

"It's safe to say there are probably several people tuning in right now. Dead, yes, but curious as ever."

"That's insane." She lowers her voice. "I'd love to tell my grandfather about this, you know? He'd eat it up."

For some reason, I think of Evan. I dismiss it. "Give me the goss on Joe, and don't leave anything out."

Chapter 36

Help at last

My neck's cricked when I wake up.

Grace and I are still on top of the rocky ledge. Lucky for Grace, I did not fall in. Or off. That's probably why my neck's sore. From trying to keep in the safe zone. The ledge is narrower than I thought.

A discomfort trick tracks over my skin, gifting me an unwelcome rash of gooseflesh. My mind's immediately leaping to worst-case scenarios. Breaking bones. Rabid bears. Freak storms.

My phone's dead too. Did it blue tick? I don't know.

I steady my rising panic.

We did not fall in. We're okay. Everything is going to be okay.

Joe's sneaker is easier to spot in the early morning sun.

"I think he's unconscious," says Grace, who has levered the top half of her body down to get a better look.

"That's not good."

"No."

"We can head back, though. Now it's light."

We don't get far.

Officer Michaels, now in khaki green and what looks like camo pants, meets us on the rocks. He's not alone.

A paramedic's weighed down by a large pack.

"You might need a rope to get him out," I say, relieved to see help is here. "He's stuck in the underground cave."

"There's no underground cave. Didn't I tell you to stick with the search party? You're in real trouble. Directly disobeying an order."

Maybe he'd give me extra English homework as punishment. I keep my concentration on my footing. If I thought getting up here was a challenge, I was woefully unprepared for the journey back.

"Young lady, you have an attitude problem."

Says the man who can't say thank you. We found Joe. And he was where I said he'd be. What an ungrateful jerk.

He's on his walkie-talkie. "Missing students found, including missing male."

"Joe's unconscious," pipes Grace. "And it looks like his leg's broken."

If looks could kill, Grace and I would be joining the Pinedale High ghost squad.

Officer Michaels barks over the static. "Have the aerial team ready on standby."

Rocky by rock, we climb down to the clearing where the Bruno brothers vanished.

Ah! The land team is on standby. There are quad bikes, police, and a whole heap of guys in green, matchy-matchy with Officer Michaels, Grace's mom, in her vet's coat. And there's....

My dad.

He's in a crumpled suit. Hard to tell, but it might have been yesterday's. He's running his hand through his hair over and over. He'll force his receding hairline back even further at that rate.

"You got my message!"

"Are you all right? I was worried sick! What the hell are you doing out here?"

The switch from relief to fear to anxiety to anger back to fear unsteadies me.

"A kid went missing out here years ago. They never—"

"Found his body. Yes, yes, we know."

He wraps me in a big hug. A proper hug. The kind of hug he used to give when we were somewhere else, sometime else, before everything changed.

I cling to him. He always smells of the same soapy cologne, and it takes me straight to a safe, warm place.

"Let's get you home," he says.

Chapter 37

True lies

"I'm sorry, Lila. I haven't been there for you, and I was wrong."

This is not the lecture I was expecting.

Dad hesitates by the fridge. Will he reach for a beer? He bypasses the fridge and slips a pod into the coffee machine. He pours me a glass of milk.

I haven't drunk milk since primary school. Small steps. "You're not mad at me?"

"Oh, I'm furious. You deliberately went against the orders of a search party and went out exploring in those woods after dark. And I see there's still the matter of a kitten who is now on the books of Audrey Reynolds."

"Who?"

"The local vet."

"Well, her eye was glued shut. I can't take her to the RSPCA with a gammy eye." Defensive much?

He stares at the coffee machine. "You can keep her."

Yes! My heart does a full-on Simone Biles's triple-somersault vault. Then it takes a step back outside the mat. "For real? Like, forever, or just for now?"

"Consider yourself a pet owner. So long as you keep that litter tray cleaned. You feed her, you take care of her, you clean up after her. No fur on my suits."

I am beaming with the light of a million suns. And

more. "Done." Though, no fur on suits? Come on. That's a miracle and I'm all out of those.

He pulls up next to me, his coffee ready to go. "You could've been hurt out there. The officer says you were adamant about searching that part of the woods. Wouldn't take 'no' for an answer. He called you obstinate and disagreeable, to be fair." He takes an overly casual sip. "Did you have a Peter Jackson moment?"

It takes me a second to register. "Peter…?"

"It's your mom's and my code word. For when…you know. When she was talking to someone who'd passed over." He pushes his coffee cup away. "I never told you this, but soon after we met, she found the bodies of some kids who'd been abducted. Kids who'd run away from home and run into the worst of humans. She said their ghosts reminded her of Peter Jackson. Anytime the cops used to show up, she'd call it a Peter Jackson."

"I don't understand. The cops?"

"She used to help them solve crimes. Show them where to look. She didn't want you to be involved. Too young."

Any elation around Fuzzwhat has given over to a painful knot of frustration. "Then why did you take her to The Parks? Everything was fine before then. She'd still be here if…"

"The young man you found—"

"Joe."

"Joe. It happened to Annie, too."

Hearing him speak her name opens up fresh wounds.

He chooses his words carefully. "She used to have these visions, and the person hadn't passed yet, but they were already dancing with death, so to speak. There was this moment between this life and the next, and she found them there. Sometimes, she was too late. Those ones crippled her."

Why didn't she say anything? It's too late to ask her any questions now. There's a sorrow in me I don't think will ever leave. It's with me when I wake up, when I'm at school, when I'm at home, or even when I'm smiling or laughing, it taps me on the shoulder and says, "Hey, she's not here." Like I need a reminder.

I can never forget.

"She never said anything to me." I feel betrayed. Like there was this whole other mother I never knew. "She could have said something." A hint. A suggestion. A handy sticky note on the bathroom mirror.

"She didn't want to scare you. You're still so young. Leave that stuff to the grown-ups."

"But what if I can help?"

"So it *was* a Peter Jackson moment." His words are heavy, and each one falls like an executioner's axe on a stump. "I should've known. The cat." He's talking more to himself now than to me.

"The cat? You mean, Fuzzwhat?"

"It's a portal from this world to the next. That's what your mom used to say."

"There's no such thing as the cat distribution system. That's what she used to say to me." And now he's telling me that it's not an accident. That it's some kind of...divine intervention? A preordained meeting? Kismet? Destiny?

My father finishes his coffee. "It's complicated."

"There's no such thing as complicated. You just don't want to talk about it."

He looks at me with an open expression. "No, of course I don't. This was not what I wanted for you."

"And all that talk about getting me tested."

"I'm sorry. When the guidance counsellor told me what you'd said, showed me that video...I panicked. It was your mother all over again. I don't want the school to have any reason to think you're anything other than a regular teen."

Well, that was debatable.

There's so much to digest I need antacid to stop from burping up more ugly truth. "So that's why she was happy to help those people? At The Parks? She thought they wanted to access the space of those who were..." What was his expression? "...dancing with death?"

"She thought she could help more people. More kids, specifically."

Peter Jackson. Running from home.

Joe. Running from his parents' expectations.

Sam. Running from small-town bigotry.

Evan. Running from his so-called friends.

All caught in that gap.

"Give me a second." He pushes from the table and disappears upstairs.

It's the most we've talked in months. Properly talked. He's given me plenty of lectures, don't get me wrong. He's always got time for those.

Dad's feet are heavy on the floorboards. He's scratching around in his unopened crates and suitcases.

When he returns, he's holding a book.

It's my mother's diary. I can tell from the purple feather she bought at a farmer's market a few years ago sticking out the spine. "She wanted you to have it. To help you. It was supposed to be part of your eighteenth birthday gift."

I take it from him. She'd had it bound in purple faux suede, a chunky diary, old-fashioned, no lock.

It's addressed to me.

Funny how really important moments are often in the most mundane places. You expect them to be glittery and shiny, with perfect hair and excellent teeth in a magical setting with unicorns and fairies or something.

But it's the half-furnished kitchen with old peeling wallpaper, me in my pajamas, and a food delivery app pinging to let us know it's on the way.

The first entry reads, *Dear Baby*. She's been writing this diary to me since before I got here. The tears rush and swell. Every word is a blur. There are maps, sketches, warnings, advice.

It's full of her experiences of the other side, the ghosts she'd met, the things she'd learned. There's even an entry on Pinedale High. "A ghost magnet", she's written.

I can hear her in every word. Her humor, her kindness, her no-nonsense when she's pissed.

The last entry is dated the day she died.

"Dear Lila,

Know that more than anything, I love you. I have always loved you, and I will carry that love for you through to what lies ahead.

I still don't know what's on the other side. The ones you'll meet? They're stuck. One foot in the living, one in the dead. I've seen glimpses of that other world, and it's always shaped by them.

I've shared everything with you. If the answers are not in these pages, then they're out there for you to discover.

203

The world's changed since I was your age, and it will continue to do so.

Be yourself. Don't hide. One day, the world will catch up.

Live, Lila. Live your dreams. And trust me when I say love is always real, it's always there, and it's always with you.

Always.

Forgive me."

After that, only blank pages.

My father's arms hold me close and tight. Fuzzwhat's meandered downstairs and is pawing at my ankles. I cry for a long time. Until my throat is raspy and dry like sandpaper. And I need to blow my nose and have a glass of water.

My dad also cries.

It's good.

We can start again properly now.

Chapter 38

Ping!

Reynolds!
Evan *Reynolds*!
Audrey *Reynolds*!
This time, when I wake with a start, it's a good thing.
Somehow, I don't think this is a coincidence.
A rash of gooseflesh ripples over my arm. The hairs on the back of my neck stand up. What if Grace's grandfather is Evan's brother?
The surnames check out.
The dates check out.
What if?
I wait until eight. That's a reasonable time to text on a Sunday, right?
—*Hey! Is your grandfather's name Beau?*—
Send.
No, wait.
—*How's Joe?*—
Send.
—*R u good?*—
I'm winning at life here.
No one appreciates ping, ping, ping. Three new messages at eight in the morning and on a Sunday.
Fuzzwhat's eye is less gluey today. She's headfirst in her bowl.

My familiar. My portal to the next world. Who'd have thunk? All covered in cat pate and dry-food beard.

Ping.

It's not Grace, though, it's Jo.

—*Saw the most incredible pr of jeans. Thought of you. <3—*

I don't know how to feel. I texted her yonks ago and she left me hanging on read. Where would I even begin to describe what's been happening?

Ping. Grace.

—*Yes, Beau. Why? He's better. All good.—*

See? Much better texter than me. One text, multiple thoughts.

My thumbs cannot type fast enough.

—*U won't believe this...—*

Two seconds later, I'm heading down the road to Grace's, still in my pj's with my dad's football jacket on top.

She's on the veranda holding out a cup of coffee, still in *her* pj's, an old-school photo album under her arm. "You want? I can drink it if you're not into it?"

"So into it." I take the mug from her, grateful for the caffeine boost. "Did he mention a brother?"

"It's the reason for his obsession with the school." She drops her voice to a whisper. "Better keep it down, though. Mom's day off, and she'll rip me a new one if I wake her."

We sit on the porch swing. It's antique, creaks like a haunted house, and peels old paint with every move. I love it. It's like being transported into one of those movies where the city girl goes back to her hometown and marries her childhood sweetheart, who has a carpentry business.

Grace opens up the album that's yellowed with age. "Here's the two of them, see?"

It's Evan. My friendly ghost. Not in his leather jacket, but with the same blond wave, the same scowl. To say I'm excited is the understatement of the year. It's like solving some giant decades-old mystery. All the pieces lining up, slotting in, making sense—that's the best bit. The clarity after the blur. Or the Pinedale Swish.

I pat Evan's picture with my pointer finger. "Grace, this is the same Evan who helped us find Joe. I. Shit. You. Not."

"The one on the rocks?"

"Yep." Now that I remember it, they both scaled those rocks with the same ease. Maybe it's genetic? "The very same one. This is amazing. Your great-uncle shoving away those bullies, standing up for you. That's a heck of a ghostly guardian to have."

Grace looks crestfallen. "And I missed all of it. Why can't they make glasses that can see ghosts? My great-uncle! Wow!"

She continues to flip through the pages. The two boys are fishing, goofing about in their father's car, shuffling playing cards. "He looks the same age as me, though. A great-uncle who's always fourteen."

"I think he was a bit older than that." There's an article about the great Pinedale fire. It looks like it's been braised in coffee. "Was that the fire he died in? The fire of '53?"

"Yeah. They thought they'd evacuated the gym, but there were three guys still in there."

"Eugene and Charlie Bruno, and Evan. He went back to look for his brother."

There's astonishment in Grace's voice. "Those are

the names here. Look!" She traces her finger under the fine print. "Gramps said he wasn't even at the school. Their mother had grounded him that afternoon. He said Evan was allergic to anything that looked like PT, so why was he even in the gym…"

"How's your grandfather doing now?"

She sighs. "Some days are better than others. He'd kill to know what you're telling me now, but he'll probably forget it. Or not know what I'm talking about in the first place."

"That sucks."

There's a memorial photo of Evan. "Gramps said he ran with the wrong crowd. Got into trouble a lot, drank, that kind of thing."

"Teenager."

"Yeah. Guess he never had the chance to grow out of it."

I consider this. "No, I think he did. He has. Can I borrow one of these photos of your grandfather? When he was older?"

"Sure." She flips through to a photo of his graduation. "This is a good one. Look how handsome he is." The film covering the page is as brittle as a spider web. "Do you think he's still at the school because he wants to make sure Gramps's okay?"

"Could be."

"If he helped me, then he's gone full circle, you know? Then he can go to the other side. It's weird how of all the ghosts at Pinedale, the one who helped us is related to me."

"All the ghosts at Pinedale."

I skimmed through the page in my mother's diary dedicated to Pinedale High. Talk about ghost central.

High supernatural activity, is how she described it. A portal between the two worlds. A space where the veil is nano-thin. And it ends on the borders of those woods. So the woods are haunted too.

And that's where my dad decided to move us to.

I get that it's his hometown. But really?

He admitted that he did not think his decision through.

You think?

"I wish Gramps was how he was. He'd be straight to the school right now asking you to find his brother and then have you play messenger. He always swore he could feel Evan around that school. Near the gym mostly. He said it was a feeling in his bones. Turns out, he was right."

"Dead-on. I met him on my first day. Well, *meet* is the wrong description. Let's say I was made aware of his presence."

"This is amazing. I can't wait to tell him. He'll be so stoked. He even had this transmitter thing he'd bought off the internet to try and track paranormal activity. It registered nothing. And then you arrive here at Pinedale in my history class."

If you told me my heart had filled with helium and been lifted high into the air to bob among the clouds, I'd believe you. My dad and I are finally talking true, I have my own kitten, I have new friends, and I have a head start on this ghost thing.

"To be fair, that was my father's doing, nothing to do with me. Parent moves, you follow."

Grace shakes her head. "It's the only thing he's ever wanted. To connect to his brother. It proves that even if you wait a lifetime, your wishes can come true. It's never too late for the stars to align."

I sip my coffee. This feels far too philosophical for a Sunday morning. "How's Joe doing?"

"I'm going to the clinic this morning. You should totally come along."

"And be a third wheel? I'm good. Thanks, but I need to start catching up on my studies. There are large gaps of no overlap."

Talking to ghosts or not, I still have to get through school. And Algebra. And Social Studies. And English.

"You could always ask a ghost to help you during a test or exam," Grace teases.

"Are you, Grace Hanratty, suggesting I cheat?"

"Just saying…And your dad? Was he okay with you?"

"Better than expected. We talked a lot."

Grace nods. "It's a good day."

It is.

Chapter 39

Tying up loose ends

Sam's sitting on the bathroom vanity, leaning against the wall. I'd swear from the way they're holding their hand an imaginary cigarette is in play. "Hey chickaboo, what's a-cracking?"

"You wouldn't believe me if I told you."

"Try me. I've seen some wild things in my time." They're twisting their hair round their fingers in coils.

I inhale deep and extra. "You have to come with me, though."

Sam's eyes narrow, their shoulders hunch, and they pull their arms into their body. "I don't think I want to go out there."

"What if I told you Chad is nowhere to be seen, and even better, you won't see him in these corridors ever again."

"I'd say that's great news, but really, who are you kidding?"

"You have to trust me on this one. He's not out here. Neither is his sidekick, Bozo."

"Chaz."

"Same difference."

They pull their shirt sleeves over their hands in an exaggerated motion. "You don't know what those guys are capable of."

"I do."

From out of my pocket, I take a piece of pale-pink ribbon. I've singed it at the ends so it doesn't fray. It's not the same one they lost all those years ago. I know that. Sam probably knows that. It's close enough, though. I place it between the sinks in front of the mirror.

Sam's holding their wrist. "Where did you find that?"

"Out in the woods. Down a ravine."

Sam looks straight at me. "Now, who told you to go looking out there?"

I shrug. "Intuition, I guess."

"Right."

They run their fingers over the ribbon with an intense reverence as though all the universe's mysteries were lodged in its threads. "It's the last thing I remember. I couldn't feel my legs, couldn't move my arms, but that was nothing compared to the panic I felt when I reached for...*this*, and it wasn't there." They sigh. "It wasn't there anymore."

The ribbon remains where I left it. They make no move to pick it up, to tie it to their wrist, or even to put it in their pocket.

"At first, I didn't think I was dead. You don't want to think that. That it ended. That that was all of the living I was given." They slide off the vanity and peer closely at the ribbon. "Thank you. This means more than you will ever know."

"You're welcome."

"I came straight to the school. And you know who was waiting for me? Chad. And his friends. Drinking and playing the fool like it was nothing. Like I was nothing. I can still hear him laughing. I don't want to see him, living out there. Not after all he took from me."

"I promise you he's not out there. And I doubly promise you that you want to see the surprise I have for you."

They retreat back to their side of the sinks. "I'm not sure I want to. I'm not ready to come out yet."

"It will only be to me. If you don't like it, we'll come straight back."

"Pinky swear. No—" They point to the ribbon. "Proper pinky swear."

"I swear on the pink ribbon that you can come right back here."

They jump off the sink. "Well, why didn't you say that in the first place?" They fluff out their hair. "How do I look?"

"A-mazing. Lit. Fire. Flames. Yass, queen."

"You're a weird one. I like you."

I hold open the bathroom door, and Sam steps through with their head held high, their chest proud.

"Why does it look different? Where have the blocks gone?" There's a stammer in their voice. "Why are all the students looking at those calculators?"

"Calculators?"

"Punching in numbers?"

"Those are cellphones." I yank mine out. "See? It's a smartphone."

"You're walking around with mobile phones? Like the ones they have in cars?"

"Cars don't have phones. You can't use your phone in the car, though. You'll get fined."

Sam gawps. "Have I walked into the future?"

"A little. I think we turn here."

"Where are we heading?"

"The library."

"It's up those stairs to the right." Sam shines up an imaginary badge on their lapel. "My first year here, I was a library monitor. Packed and stacked books, hid amongst the shelves, helped the kids with the index cards."

"Brace yourself," I warn them. "It's not how you remember."

Turns out the library is in exactly the same place.

Sam stops in their tracks. "What? Are you kidding? This is not the library. There are so many computers. Why are kids watching TV? Are they listening to music? Why are they wearing headphones? They've all got those clever phones."

Sam's gasping and oohing and aahing.

I usher Sam to an empty computer station near the back of the library. Somewhere quiet. I am with a ghost, after all, and I don't want to be accused of talking to myself. Again.

The first thing I do is pull up Chad's online profile. He wasn't difficult to find. "Ta-da!"

"Who's that? Is it?…Oh my God, that's not Chad."

"It is."

"Where's his hair got to?"

"Gone."

They nod in approval. "This is good. So good. Divorced. What a pity." Their smile widens. "Lila, have you read this?"

"I certainly have."

Sam's face is animated, alive, aglow with the sweet taste of karma. "Arrested and convicted of fraud. I'll say. Thirty-two counts against him. Sounds like a stand-up guy." They read off the screen. "Single-handedly responsible for bringing down a merchant bank. I don't even know what that means. A crook. A low-down dirty thief. Yeah, I know all about you, Chad." Their fingers hover over the keyboard. "How do you find out about the others?"

"Chuck their names into the search engine and see what it spits back."

"I don't know what that means, but it sounds good."

"In a second. Let me show you the surprise first."

"Chad's fall from grace is not the surprise?"

"Nah, that's a cherry on top."

I type in Sam's name. The one Grace's grandfather gave to me.

Sam is very silent. "Wait, that's me." Tears fill their eyes. "And that's my mom. I miss her. They could have chosen a photo of me without my braces. My fourth-grade class photo? Was that the best they could do? Really."

I scroll to find what I'm looking for and zoom in so Sam can read every word. "I know you wanted to go to New York. And be in fashion. That you said your family would never accept your choice?"

Sam's reading the articles, their body still. "She did that. For me?"

"She did. You got in, Sam. To the most prestigious fashion school in all of fashion. In New York City, baby. She'd submitted the application for you. You got in! And they were so proud of you."

"I got in? I had a place at, at…"

"You did."

"That was my biggest dream." They're awash with tears but their make-up doesn't smudge, no puffy eyes, no red cheeks. No wet cheeks either. "How did you find this?"

"It doesn't matter. Will you promise me you won't spend the rest of your time here hiding in the bathroom?"

"Yes, ma'am." They mock salute me. "Jailed for fraud. Ha! I'll even belly flop off the high diving board!"

Chapter 40

The End?

Do you ever get that feeling that everyone's staring at you? Weighing you up, judgy mc-judgy and then some?

I'm waiting at the top of the stairs for Grace. Yep, there's no doubt. They're whispering. Bombastic side-eye at every turn. Totally sus.

"Hey, you!" It's some kid with a mullet, full-on nineties style, and he's definitely referring to me. It's the pointing finger that gives it away.

I brace myself for another socially crippling torpedo attack.

"You turned it around!" He gives me a thumbs-up with his pinkie extended.

Good thing? Bad thing?

Sarcasm? Sincerity?

I give him a brief nod of acknowledgement.

"Good job!" says another, walking hand in hand with their girlfriend. "Our very own ghost girl."

Say what? I'm frozen to the spot. Who said what said where? Ghost girl?

That opens the floodgates:

"Pinedale High's ghostbuster!"

"Yeah, who you gonna call?"

"Seeing ghosts? That slaps."

For real? And there I was, skulking around the library. Who dropped the spoilers? They're *okay* with it?

There's no more laughing at me or calling me names—that was so cringe—or sniggering.

One kid with an emotional-support dog even slow claps.

Tomas ambles past, his camera bouncing against him in a syncopated rhythm. "Pinedale Swishes and a ghost reader? And I bet you know how to ride the London Underground, too. Show-off." He sighs. "See you in the imaginarium. A heads-up, our next project will focus on liminal spaces. So start thinking creatively."

Do I tell him the swishes and the ghost thing are related? Nah. Not yet, anyway. Liminal spaces?

Now there's the ghost I've been looking for.

Evan's kicking his heels, smoking a ghostly cigarette, keeping to the shadows.

I join him. "You want the good news or the bad news?"

He looks worried.

"I'm teasing." I dig into my stack of books and pull out the photos Grace gave me. "Your brother, Beau, lives a few blocks away. Here, look, his graduation. His wedding day. His daughter—she's a vet. And, get this, you've already met your great-niece."

That was an info dump of note.

A guy with outsize glasses scuttles past us, one eye on Evan.

I wave, and he almost trips over his shoelaces.

A ghost. Got it.

Evan's entranced. "It's been so long. Look at him, man. In a suit and tie and all."

"Oh yes, he's a historian. Well, was. He's retired now."

"Ha! The kid grew up. Retired!"

His body is tightly wound with joy. Like he's about to spring and leap and dance about. Not in those boots, though.

"I met my niece?"

"The redhead."

"Red's my niece? Cool. Cool. Yeah, I can see that. And she goes here? I'll check up on her, make sure no one gives her a hard time, or I'll give them a knuckle sandwich right in the kisser, you know?" He makes a fist, but there's no anger behind it. "A historian. Wow. Went to college."

"Taught at college."

"Oh man, my mom must've bust something at that."

It's overwhelming—the emotion. It runs from him like a flooding river breaking its banks.

When he can find his voice, he tosses out his words quickly. "Thanks. I owe you." He chucks his smoke into the nothing and walks away.

A second later, he's gone.

It's a strange feeling. All of that joy, regret, love, and pain, all in one spirit.

"Sorry we're late!" It's Grace. "We had to find a ramp. This place is not very friendly to those with different needs."

Joe's in one of those big boots and crutches. He hobbles over, Grace by his side.

They make a cute couple. Very football hero and cheerleader vibes. Predictable, yes, but there's nothing wrong with that.

I see ghosts and have a black cat.

It goes together like frozen peas and corn.

Grace hands me Joe's book bag. "It's all in here. Look at that, Lila, you're Joe's buddy now. That's hilarious. Catch up with you guys later."

Joe's glasses are fixed. No more tape holding them together. He can't quite meet my gaze. "Lila, I can't begin to thank you. In that cave…" His eyes mist over, and he readjusts his crutches. "I thought it was over. I was sitting on some dead kid's bones. And I had this…dream."

I raise an eyebrow. "Dream?"

Joe has the temerity to blush. "Or hallucination. It's hard to tell. You talked about ghosts and how you could see them. I told the paramedics…and the doctors…and the police…I was out of it. I swear."

Ah! There's the leak. My blah-dy blah.

"When I came to proper…I'm sorry…it's out there." My expression causes him to continue his confession. "I outed you. I can't take it back. And then, when Grace visited me and told me that you'd found me. It wasn't a dream, was it? Because a few weeks ago, you asked if it was normal for soil to have worms in it…"

"I might have been bluffing," I argue.

"You didn't strike me as the outdoors type. Still don't." He clears his throat. "I owe you an apology. I've been a lousy buddy. That first day, when I tripped…I was so embarrassed. Me? Tripping like that? In front of the new cool girl. I forgot my manners."

Cool girl? I like that one. Me, cool. Who knew?

"And then it happened again the next day. I…yeah. I guess what I'm trying to say is thank you. Thank you."

Poor guy, though. He's had it rough. His leg is proper strapped in. "Football season is out then?"

"There's next year. Coach says I can probably make up the lost time. It's okay. I'm not totally devastated."

"Worked out for you then?"

"In a weird kind of way. Though I can't head back to the woods anytime soon, and I swear there were some excellent samples we didn't get." He gives me a tentative smile. "I don't know how to repay you."

"You could let everyone know I'm a cool girl."

"A ghost whisperer."

"I prefer vintage fashion expert and amateur stylist."

"You got it."

My Peter Jackson story. Rescuing Joe from the void. Maybe one day I'll have a daughter and tell her all about it.

I break the silence. "It looks like season five's fi-na-lly in production."

His whole face relaxes. "A total waste. The recap for that first episode will have to be an hour long. Who's got the time for that?"

"Exactly. I can't even remember what happened in the last season."

The bell rings.

"We should properly head to class. We don't want to be late."

Joe swings his crutches to correct his approach. "A few minutes won't hurt."

"Says Mr. Punctuality."

Joe's crutches clip clip as he hurls himself along. "Time is money, as my father says."

"What does that even mean? Like you get billed by the second?"

"Yes."

"Oh." I got it right! I punch the air.

"So about our terrarium—"

"We do not need any more soil samples."

"What if we did the Pinedale High terrarium project? And tested for paranormal activity?"

"That could be interesting. But there's no such thing as ghosts." Beat, two, three, four. "Only former students with a haunting problem."

My phone pings. It's Dad. The crate's finally arrived!

It's a good day to be alive.

A word about the author…

S.F.L. Jefferies's favorite holiday is Halloween. She believes black cats are magic and loves anything dark and spooky. Oh, and writing.

She loves writing paranormal young adult stories that embrace heart, humor, and all things supernatural.

When not writing, she's a committed, if unsuccessful, cat-wrangler who enters a time warp speed anytime she works on a sewing project. Afternoons literally disappear.

Thank you for purchasing
this publication of The Wild Rose Press, Inc.

For questions or more information
contact us at
info@thewildrosepress.com.

The Wild Rose Press, Inc.
www.thewildrosepress.com